Another Sommer-Time Story

Tied Up In Knots

By Carl Sommer
Illustrated by Greg Budwine

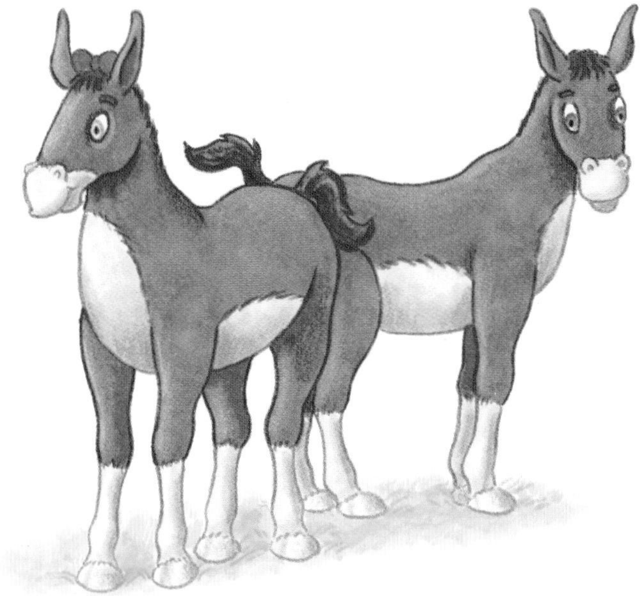

Advance Publishing, Inc • Houston

Permissions
Advance Publishing, Inc.
6950 Fulton St.
Houston, TX 77022

http://www.advancepublishing.com

First Edition
Printed in Singapore

Library of Congress Cataloging-in-Publication Data

Sommer, Carl, 1930-
    Tied up in knots / by Carl Sommer ; illustrated by Greg Budwine. –
1st ed.
        p.   cm. – (Another Sommer-time story)
    Summary: Until they see their two stubborn mules finally resolve a
behavior problem, Benny and Sally refuse to believe that sharing
could bring happiness.
    ISBN 1-57537-050-6 (lib. bdg. : alk. paper). – ISBN 1-57537-003-4
(hardcover : alk. paper)
    [1. Sharing–Fiction. 2. Obstinacy–Fiction. 3. Behavior–
Fiction. 4. Mules–Fiction.]   I. Budwine, Greg, ill. II. Title.
III. Series: Sommer, Carl, 1930-   Another Sommer-time story.
PZ7.S696235Ti 1997
[E]–dc20
                                                                    96-22014
                                                                         CIP
                                                                          AC

Another Sommer-Time Story

Tied Up In Knots

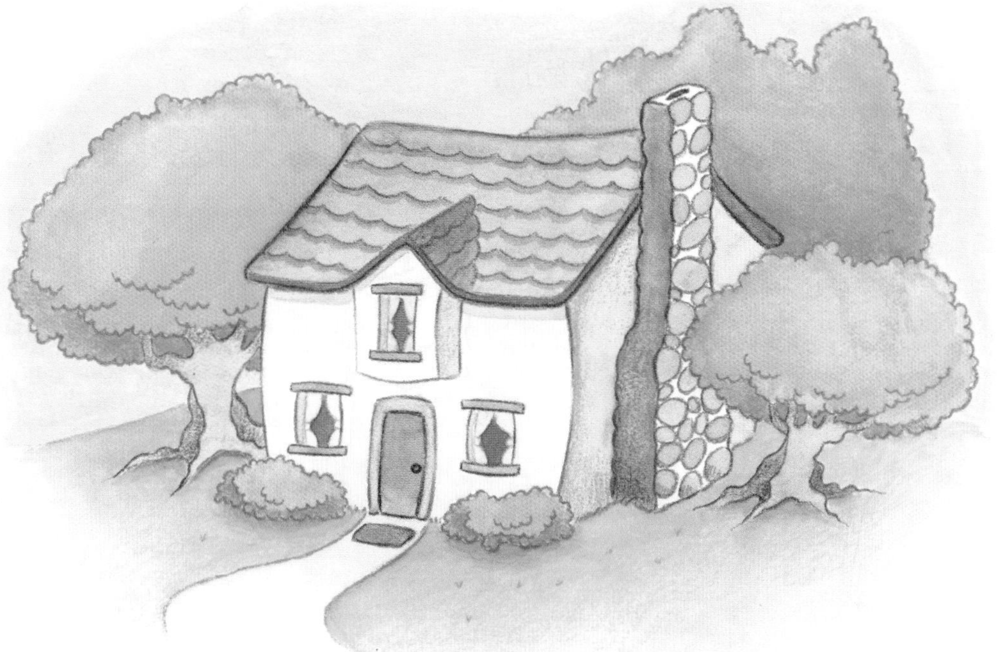

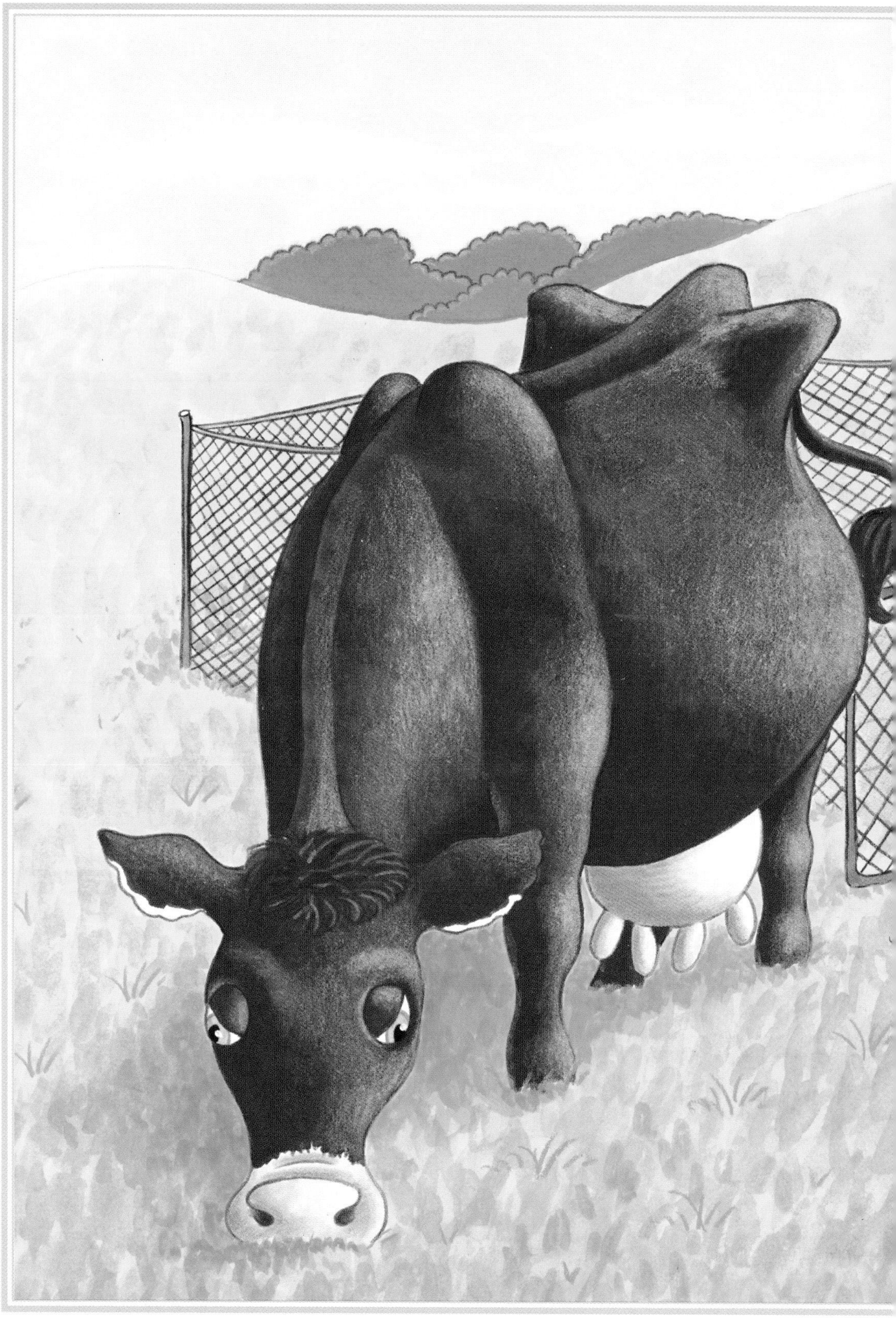

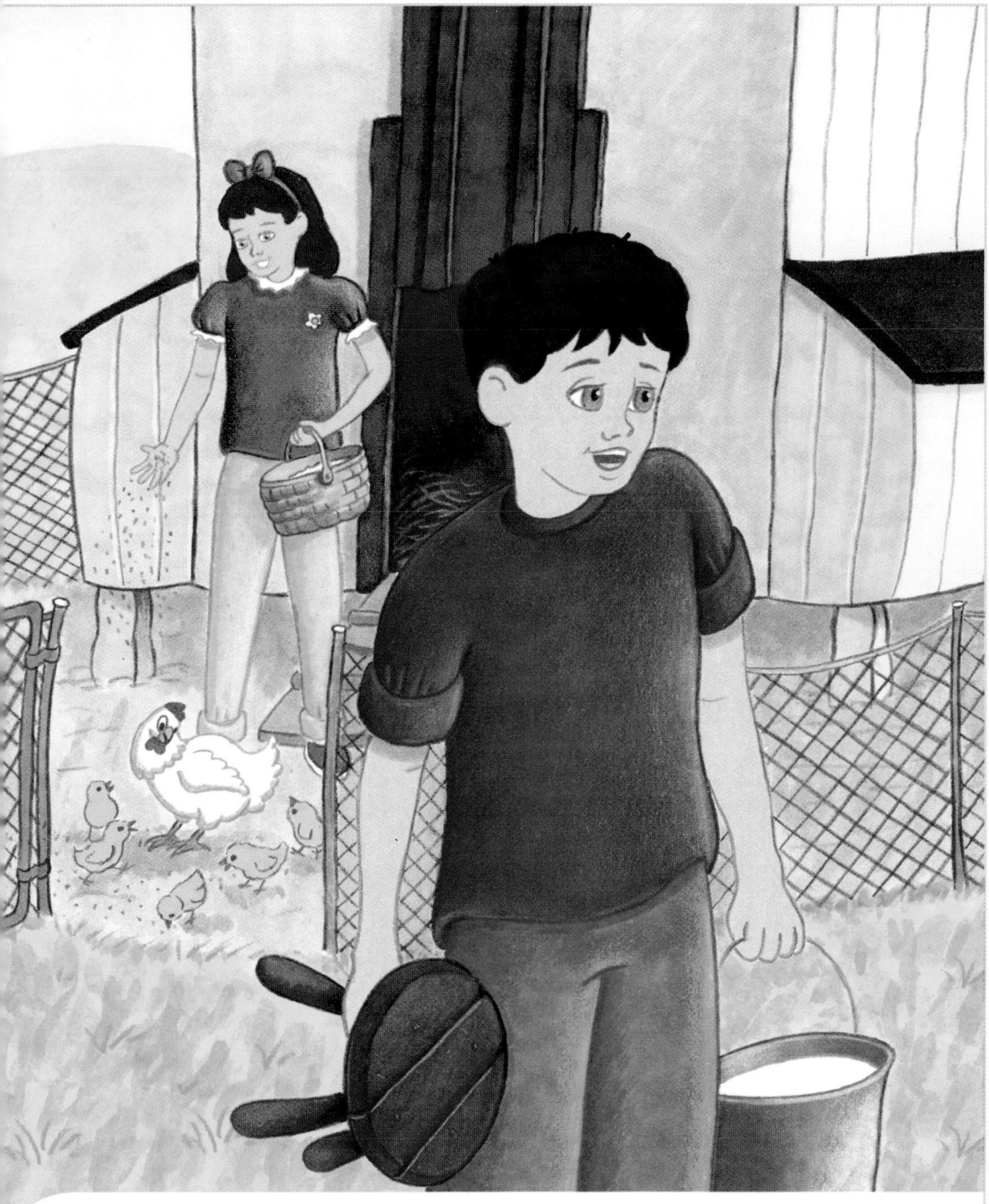

Benny and Sally liked growing up on the farm. There were lots of things to do.

First they would work...

. . . then they would play.

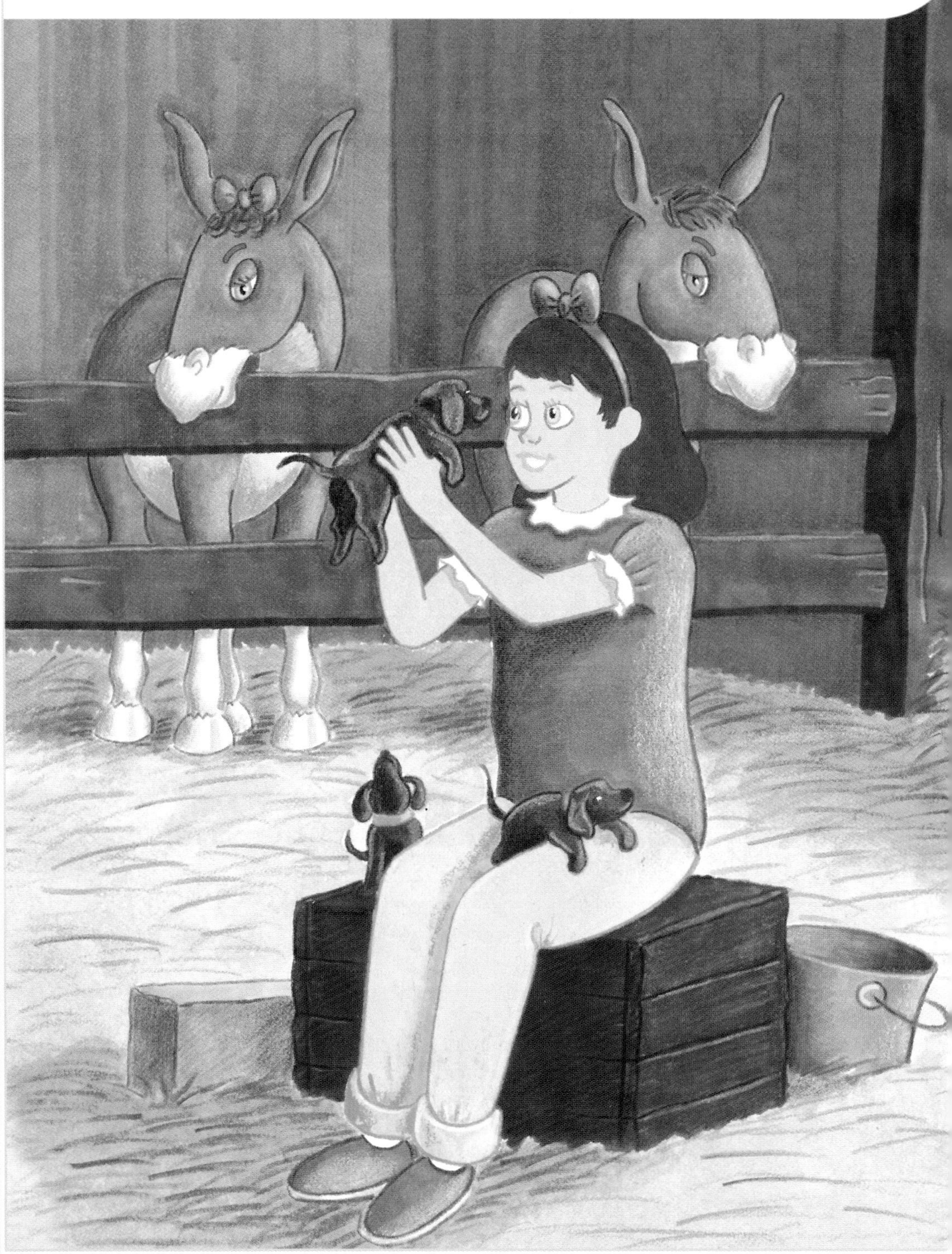

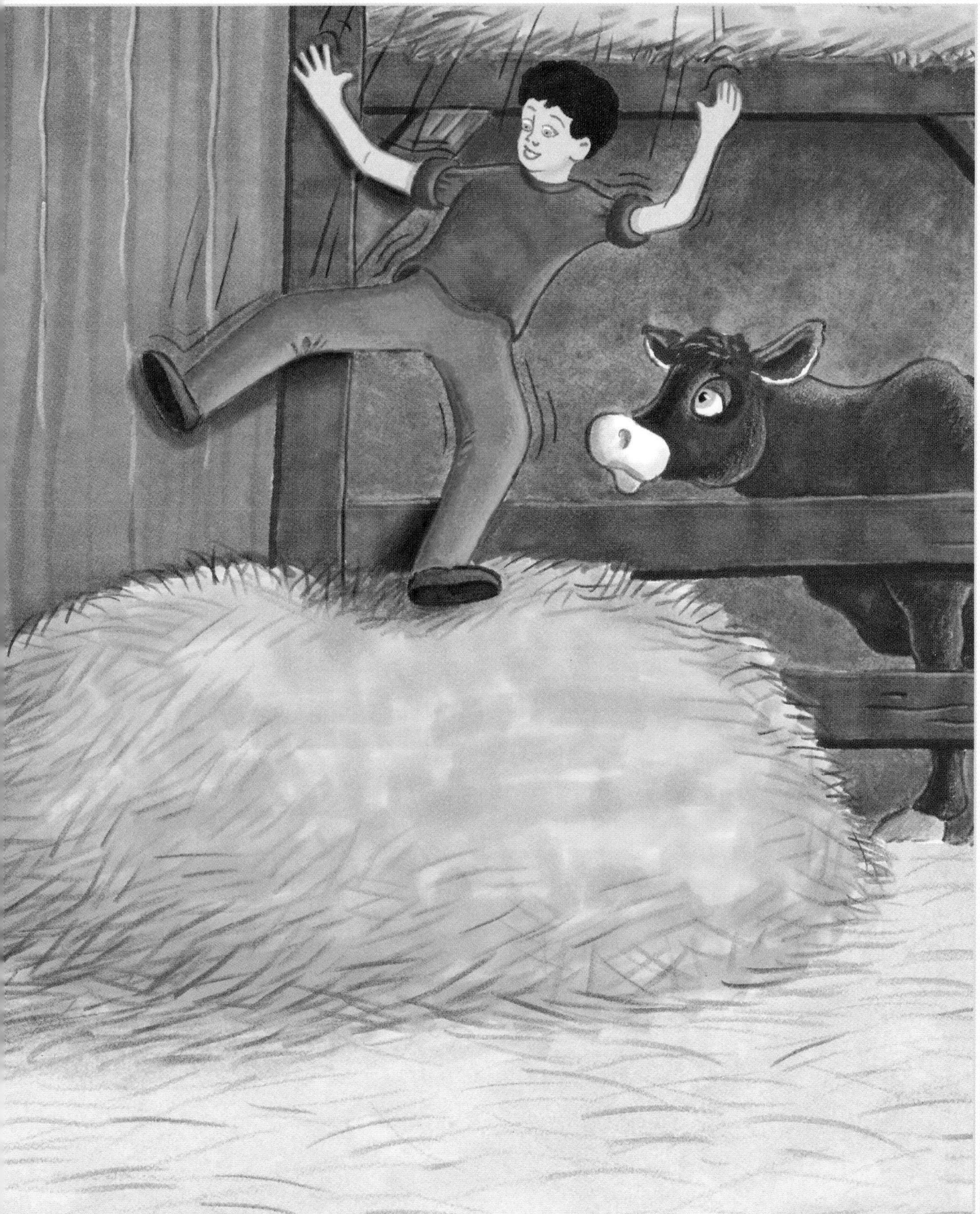

But there was one thing they would *not* do.

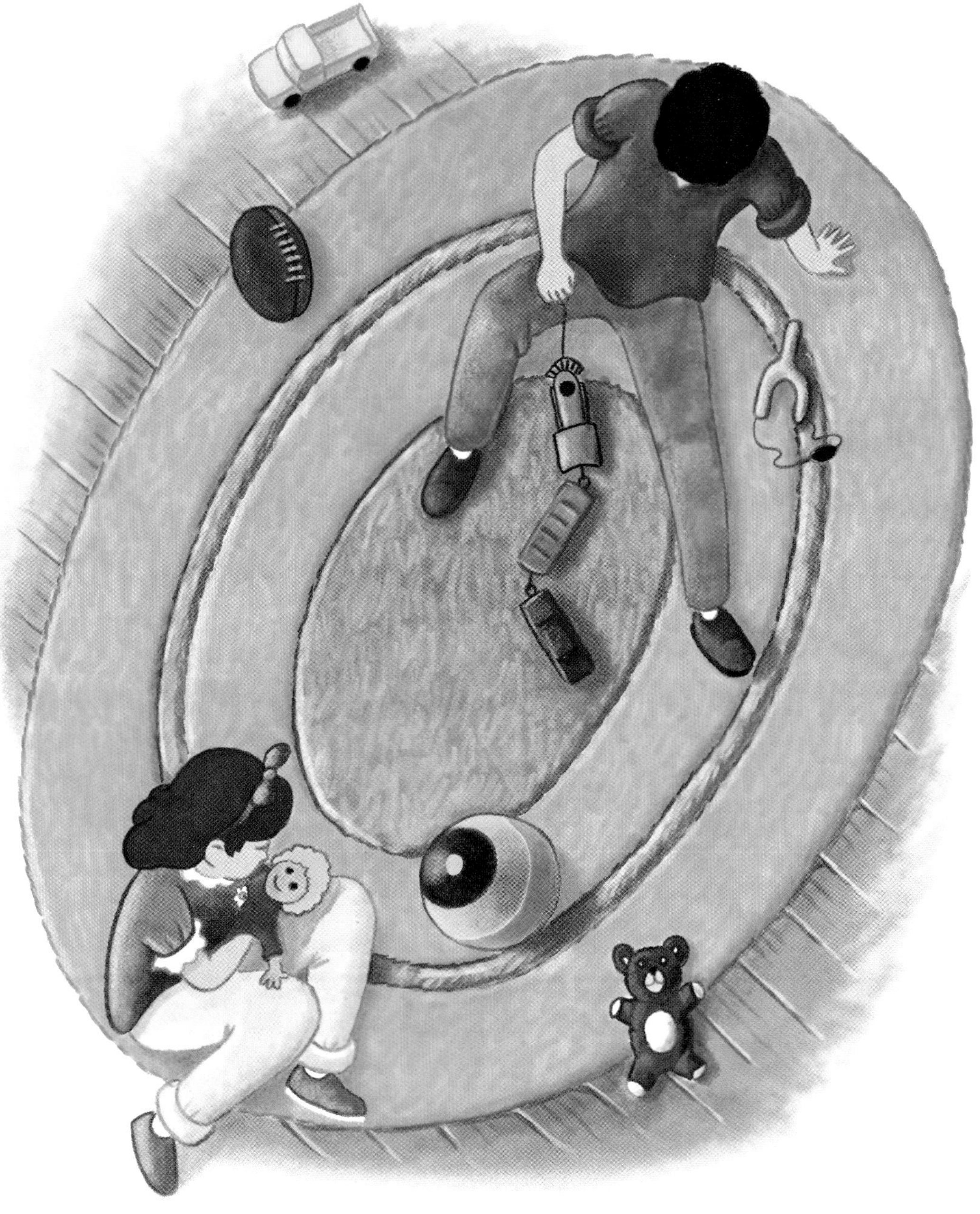

Benny and Sally would *not* share.

Only Benny could play with Benny's toys...
and only Sally could play with Sally's toys.

The same was true for their mules. *Bossy* was for Benny . . . and *Stiffy* was for Sally.

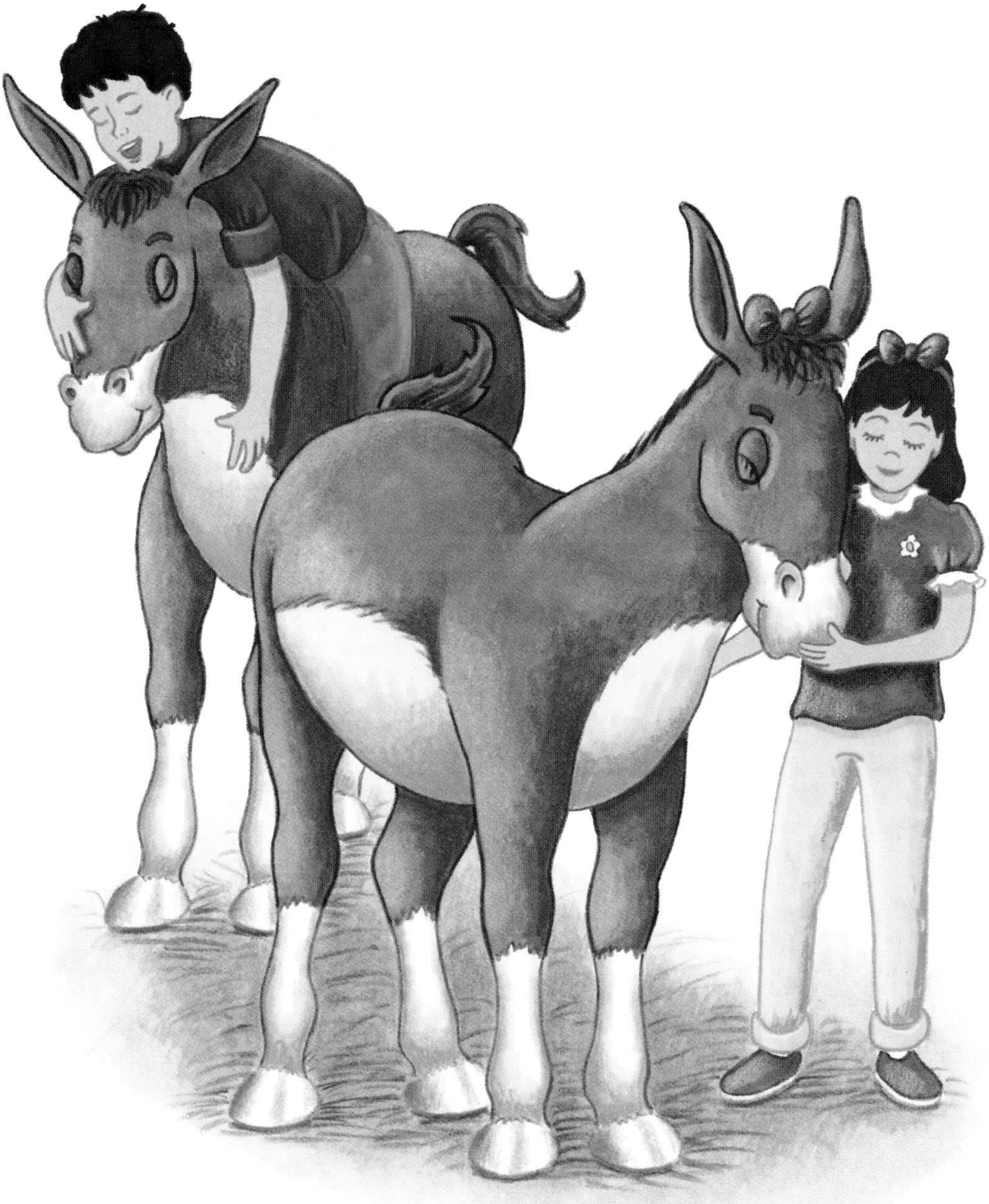

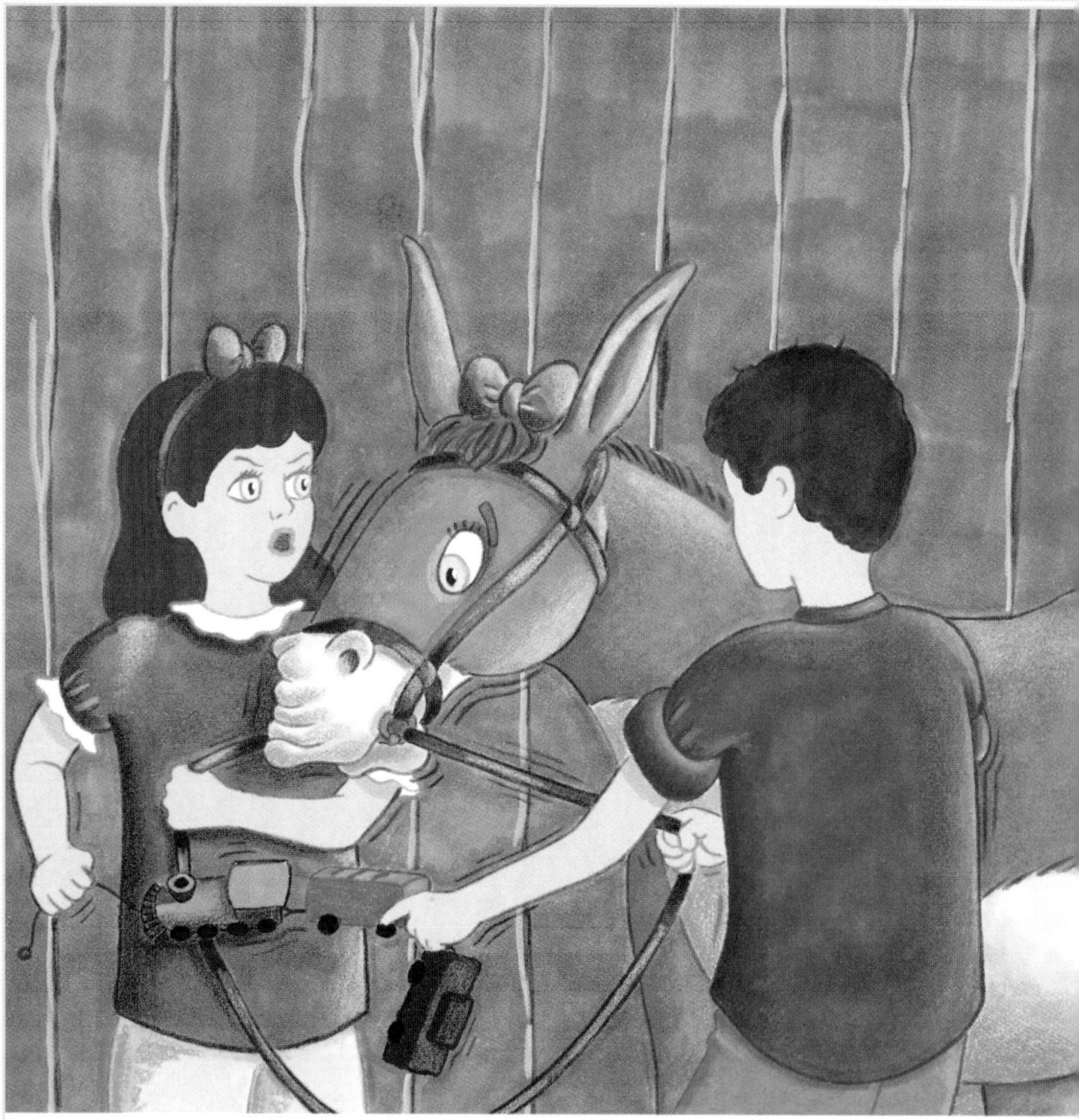

If Benny asked to ride Sally's mule, Sally would cry out, "No! That's my mule! I'm *not* sharing!"

If Sally had one of Benny's toys, Benny would grab it and yell, "Give it to me! That's *not* your toy!"

Benny and Sally just would *not* share.

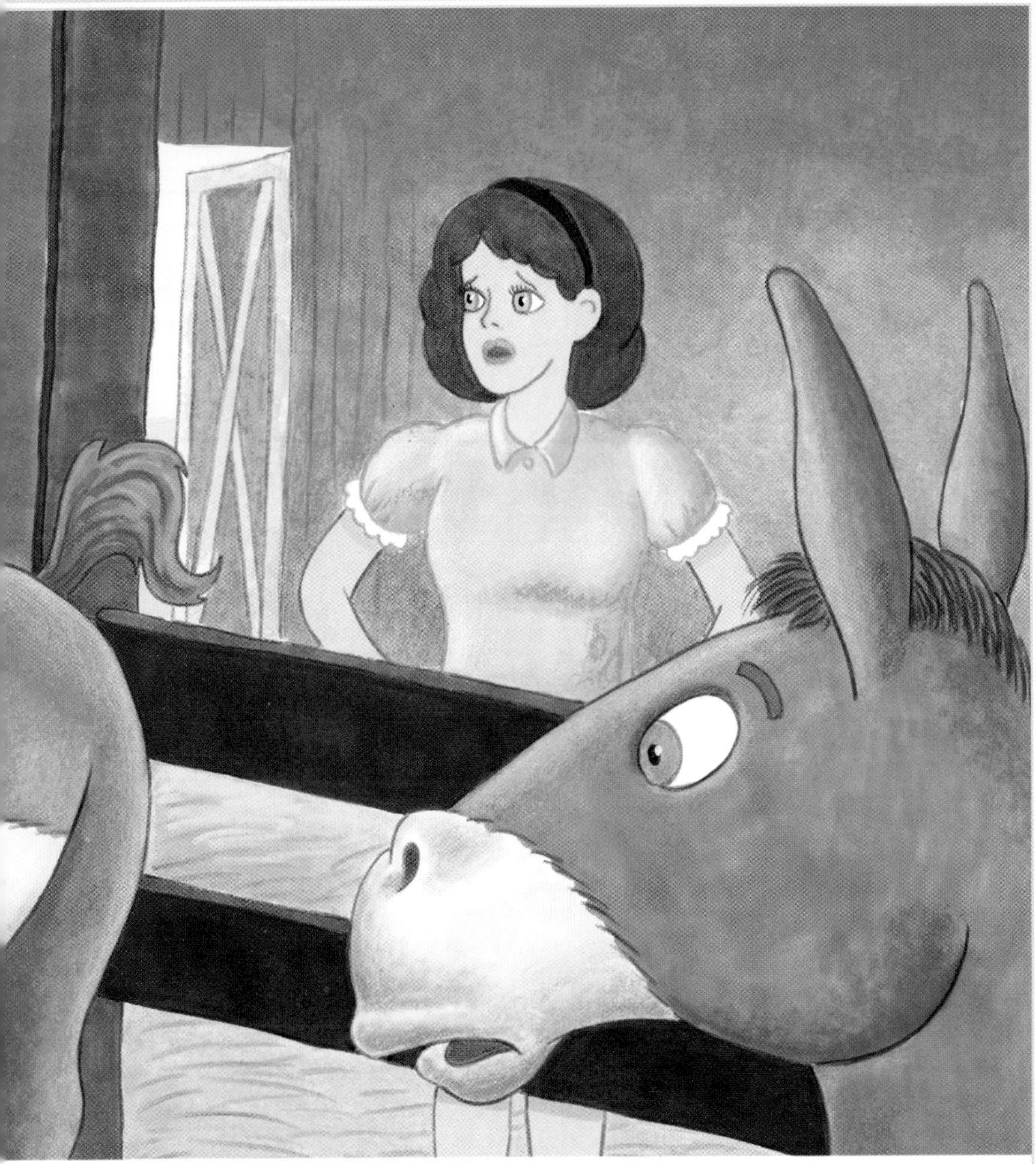

When Mom heard them yelling and fussing, she would tell them, "Be kind to one another. Remember, sharing brings happiness."

But Benny and Sally would *not* listen. They thought sharing would make them unhappy.

Benny and Sally did not know it, but Bossy and Stiffy had become just like their owners—*not* very friendly, and *not* very kind.

Once, when Sally was not around, Benny hopped onto Stiffy to go for a ride. But Stiffy *stiffened* her neck and would not move!

Sally's mule was for Sally . . . *not* for Benny!

When Sally tried to sneak a ride on Bossy, the stubborn mule dug in his feet. He was not about to take Sally anywhere—he was the *boss*!

Benny's mule was for Benny . . . *not* for Sally!

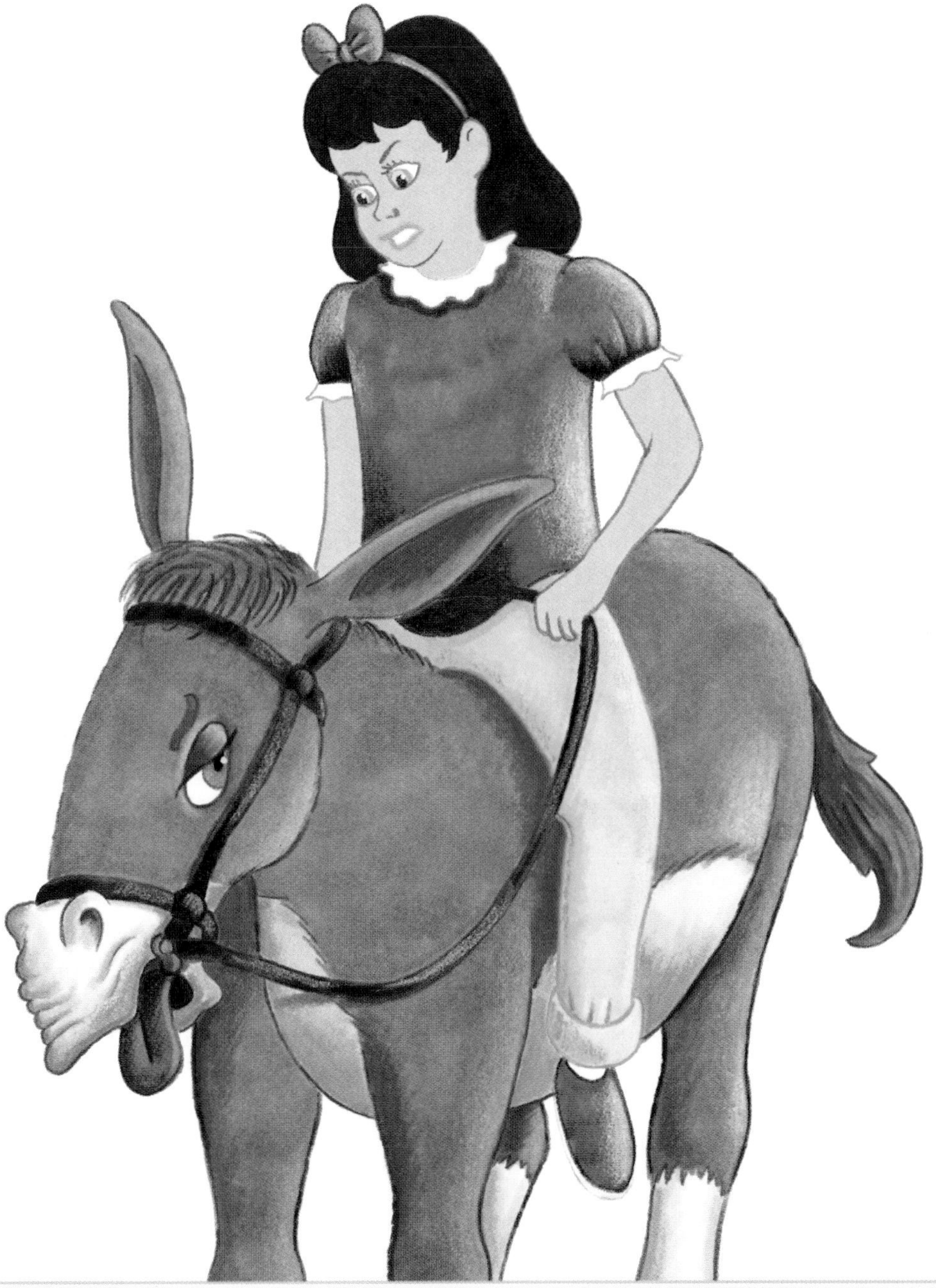

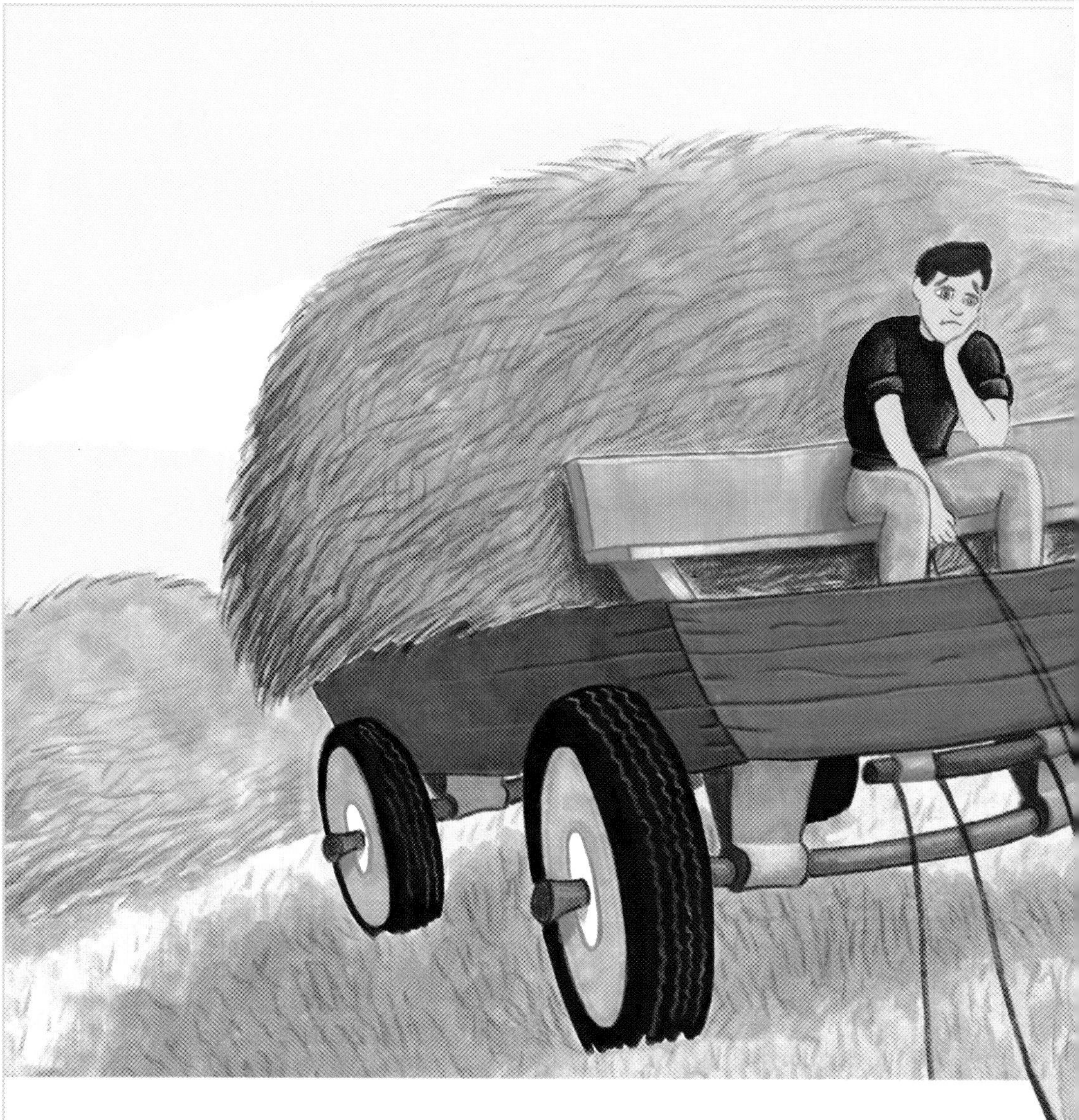

When Dad tried to use Bossy and Stiffy, the stubborn mules acted just like Benny and Sally—they would only fuss and fight. They did not want to work together and share the load.

"Haven't those mules learned yet that sharing brings happiness?" asked Mom.

"I guess not," said Dad, shaking his head. "But I think it's time to teach them."

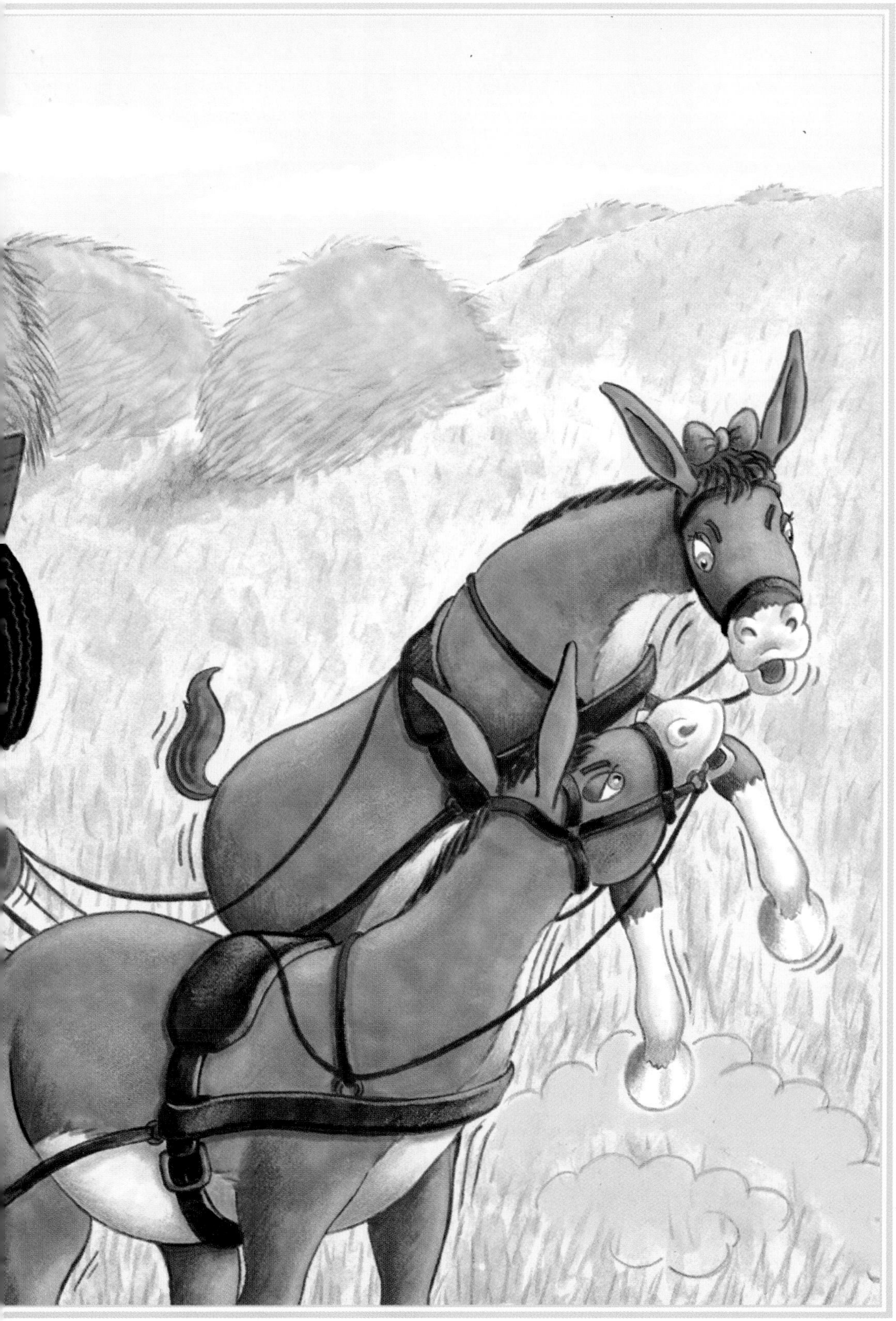

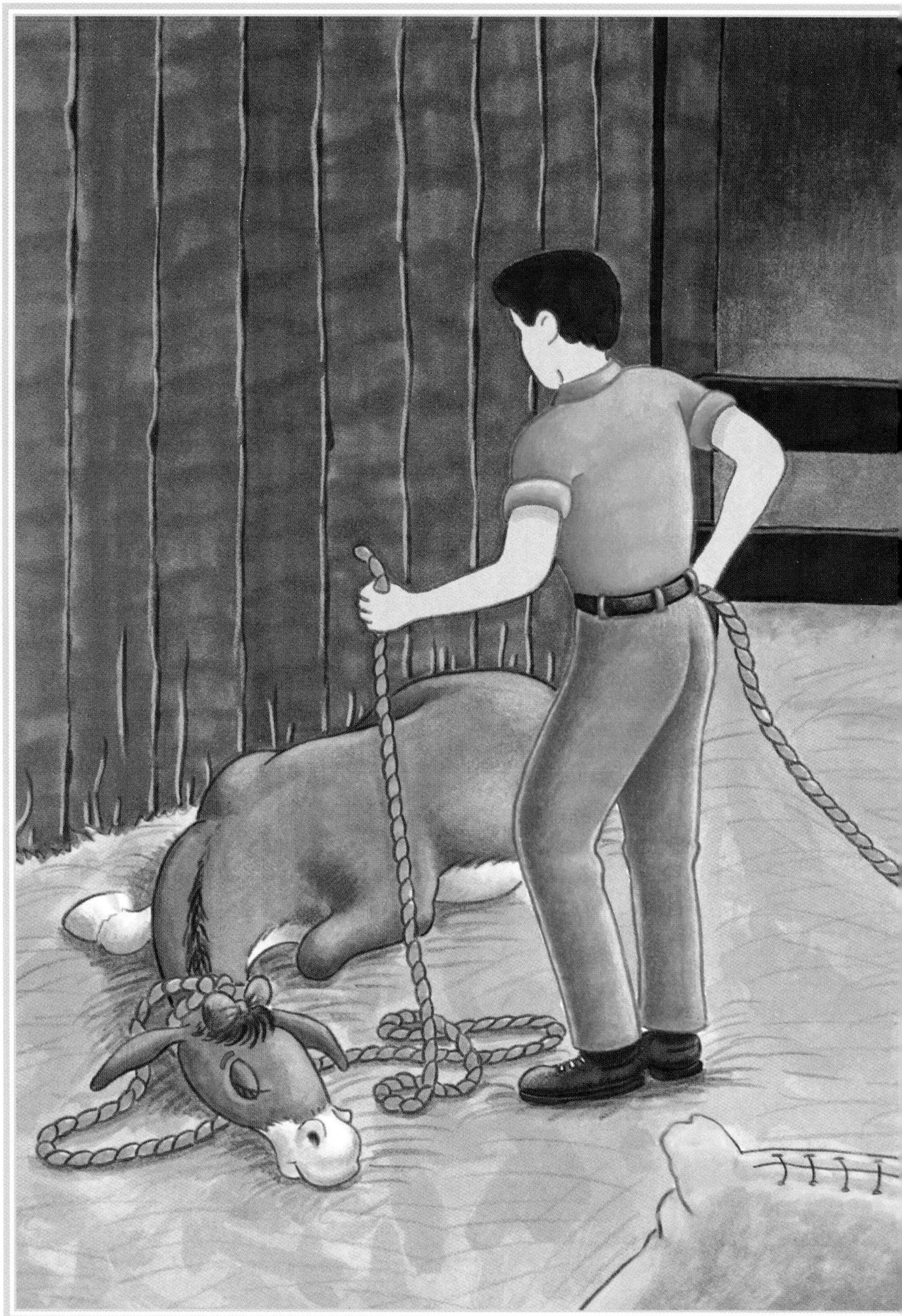

Early the next morning Dad tiptoed into the barn, being very careful not to wake the sleeping mules.

He picked up the rope that was around Bossy's neck. Then he got the rope that was around Stiffy's neck. Quietly, he tied the ends together.

Then Dad and Mom left to go to town.

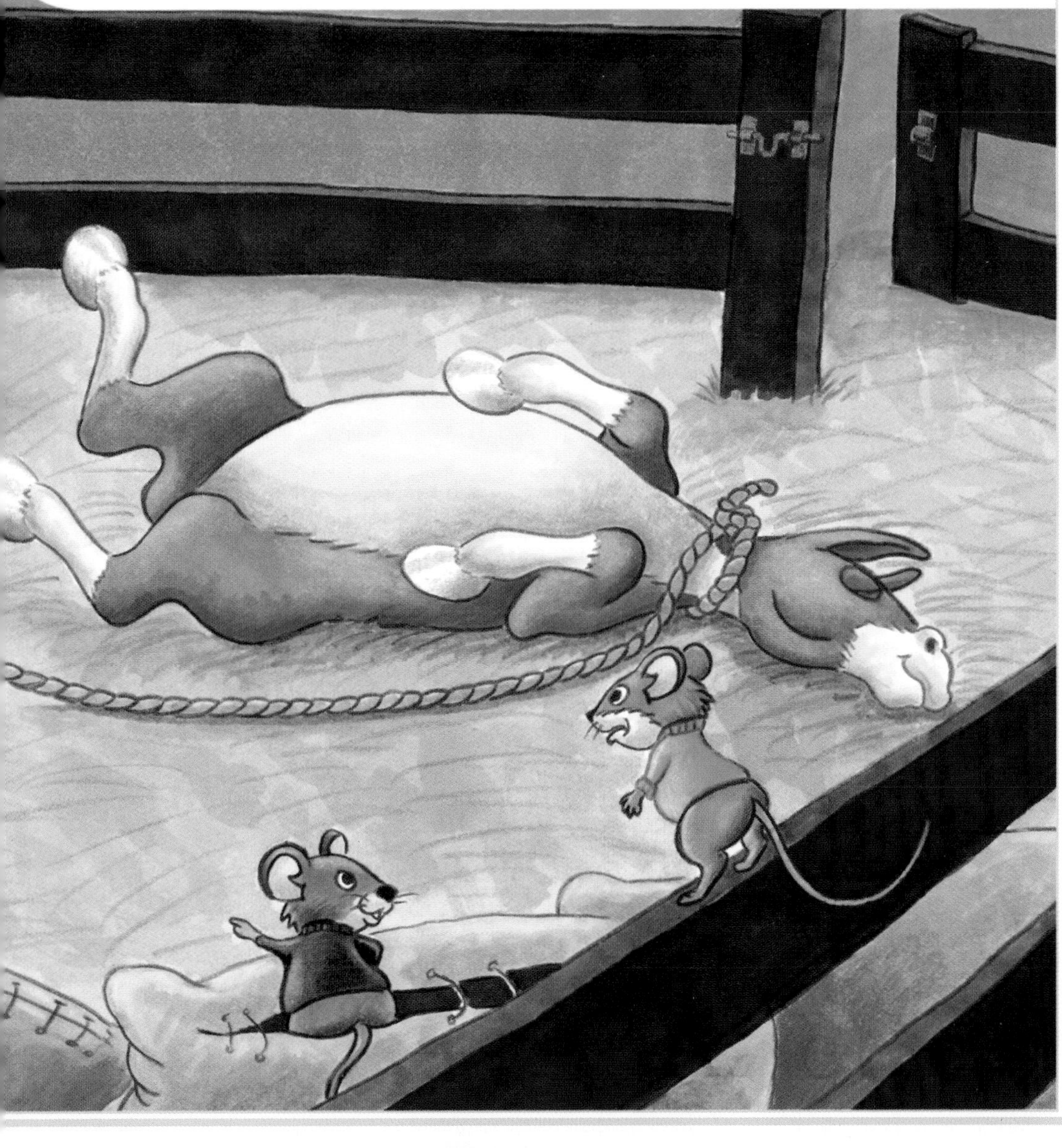

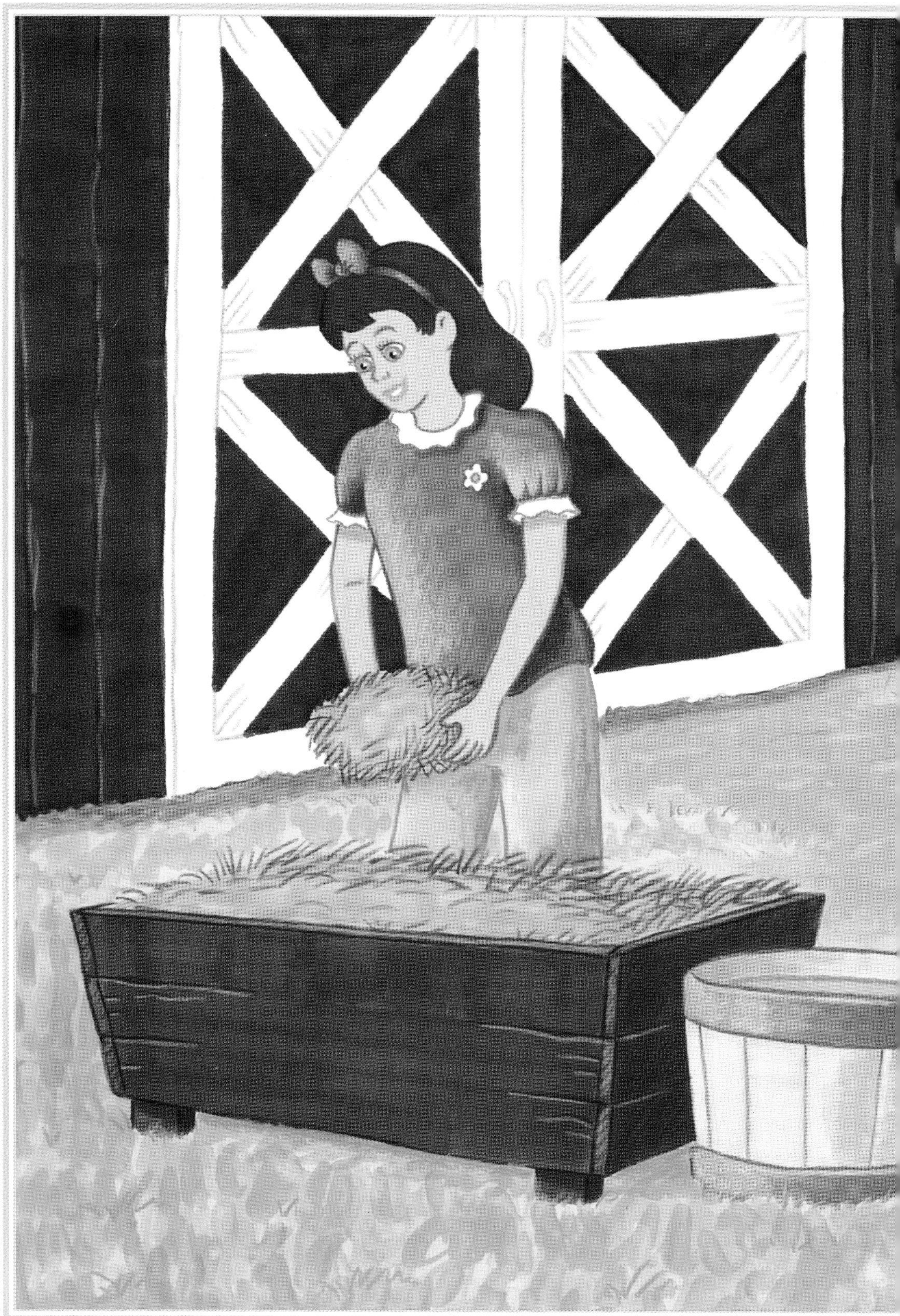

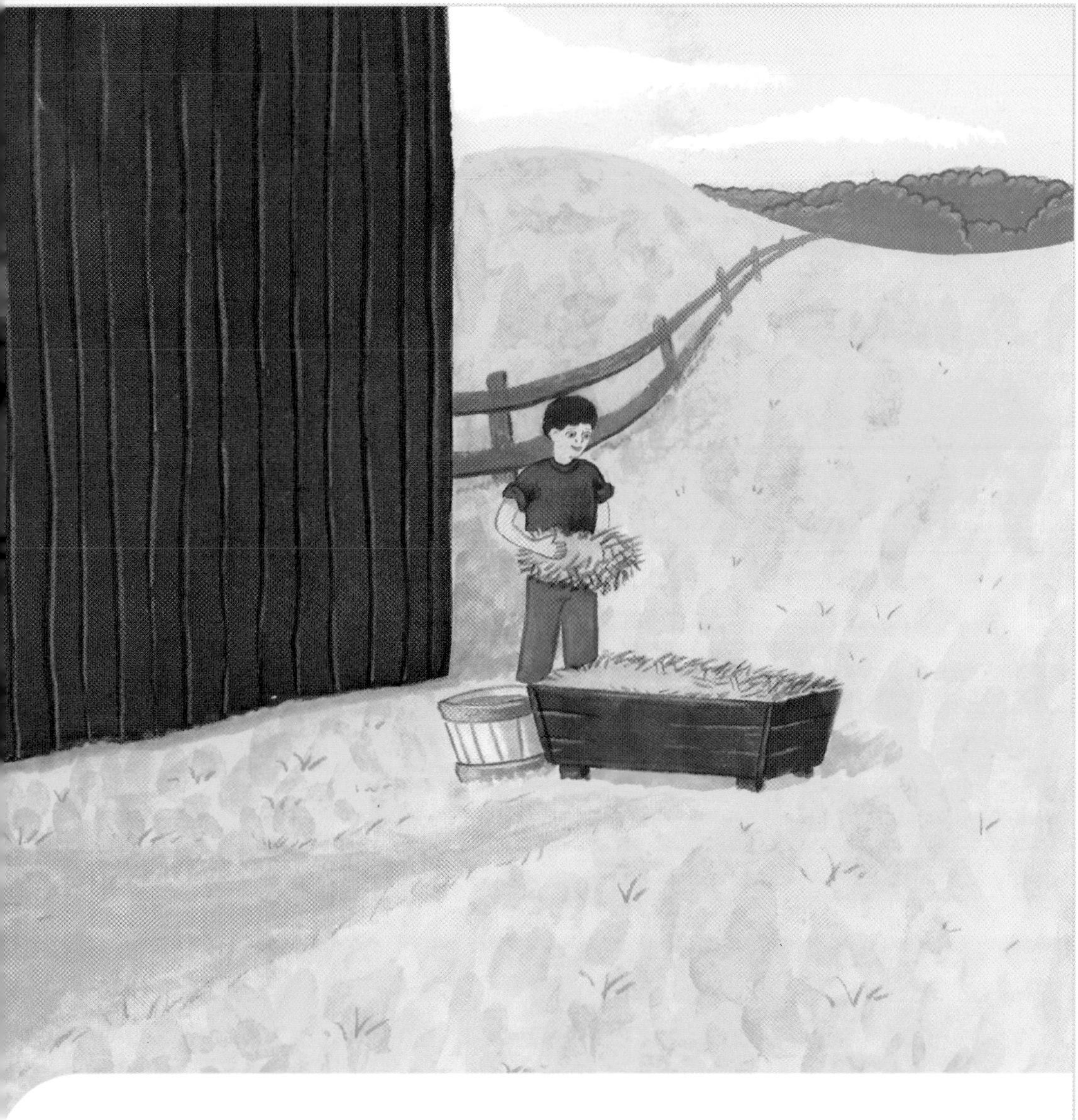

Benny and Sally began the day as always, taking care of Bossy and Stiffy.

They filled the big tubs with water and stuffed the troughs with hay.

"Here Bossy," called Benny as he opened the barn door. "Time to eat."

"Come Stiffy," yelled Sally. "Breakfast is ready."

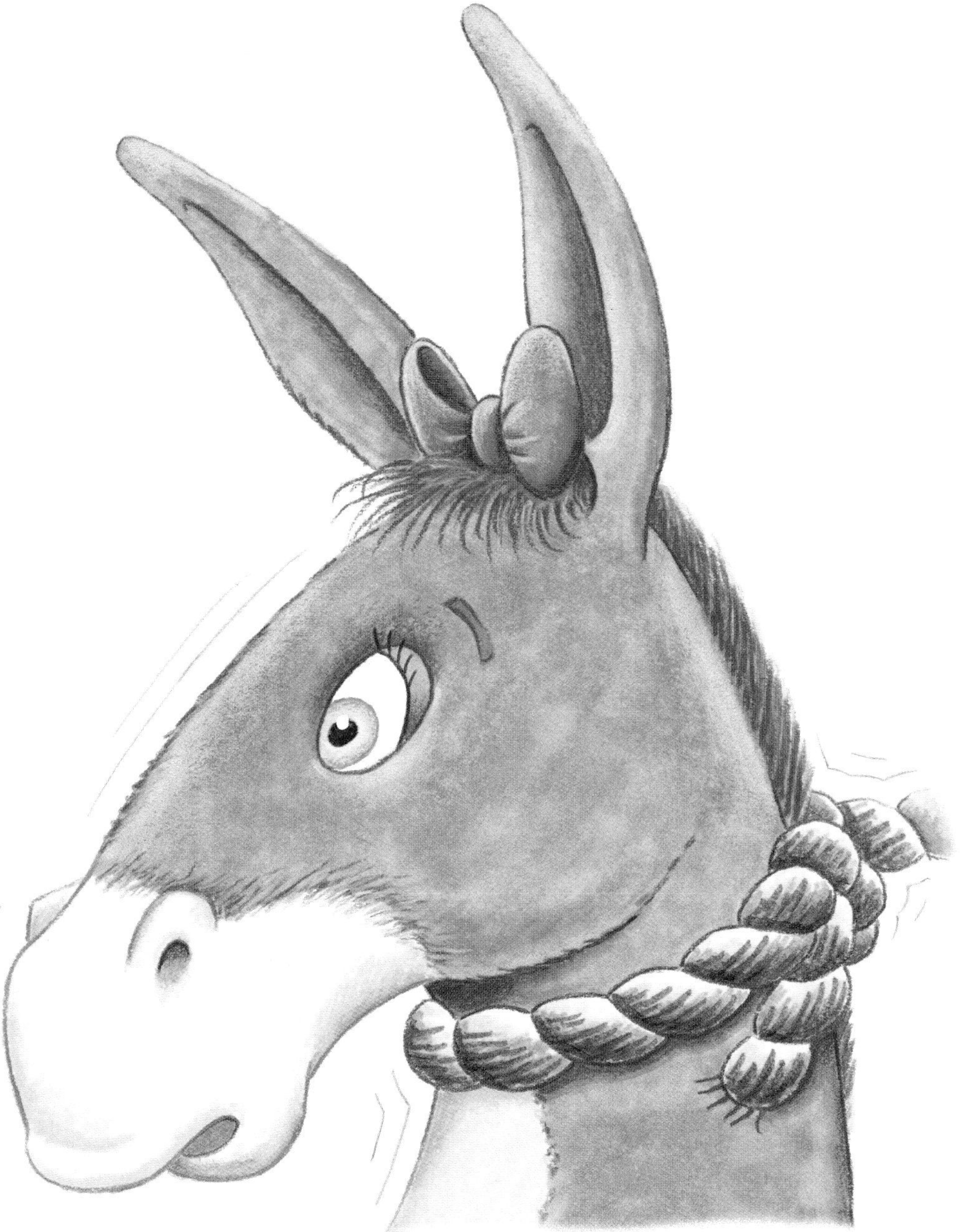

Bossy and Stiffy stretched and yawned, then headed straight for their food.

As the mules neared the hay, they felt a heavy tug at their necks. Suddenly they stopped!

"What's wrong, Bossy?" asked Benny.

Sally saw the problem. "Stiffy! How did you get tangled up with Bossy?"

"Somehow they got tied up in knots!" Benny exclaimed.

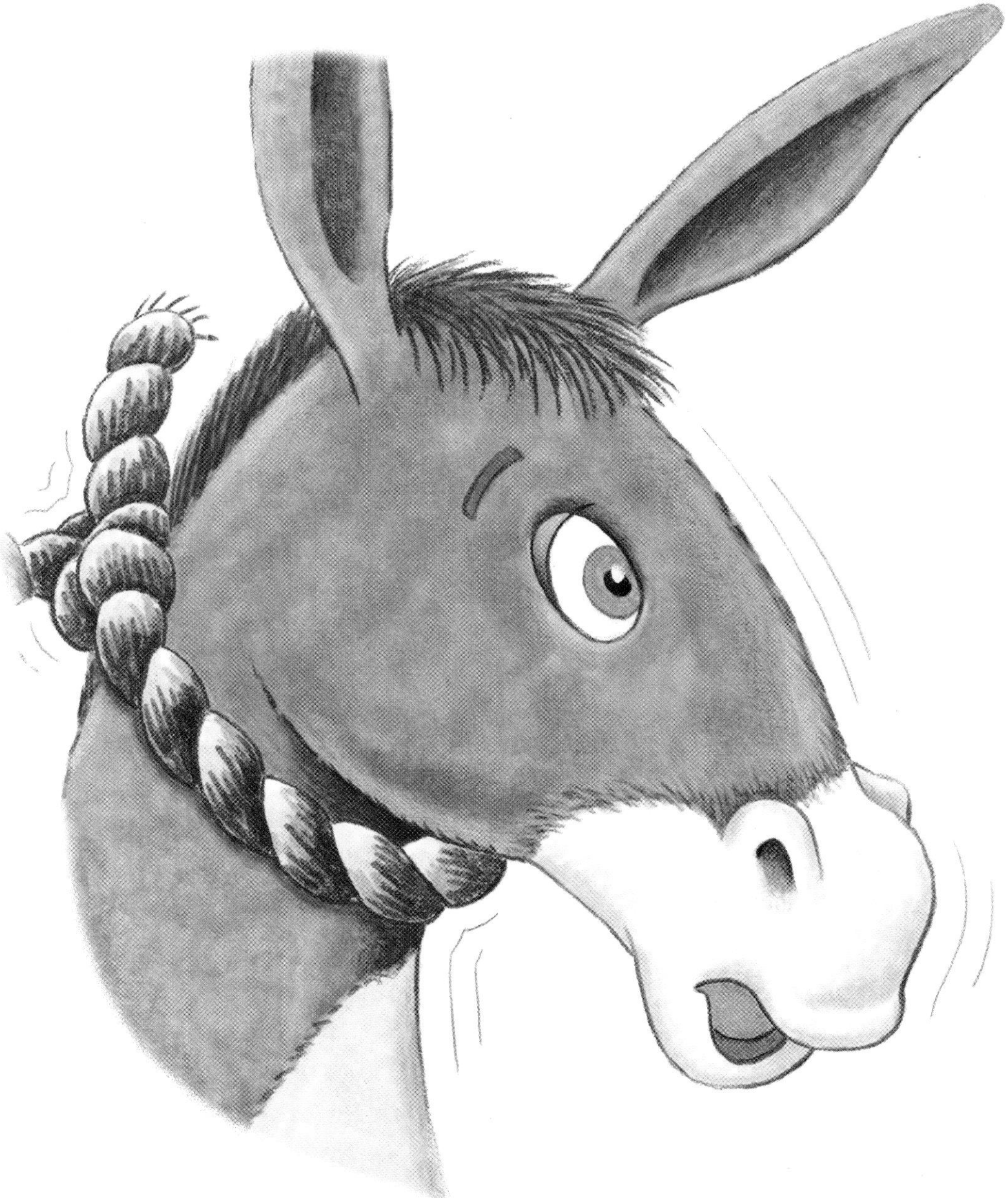

Bossy and Stiffy did not care about the rope or the knots. They were hungry . . . and they were ready to eat.

They began pulling harder and harder. But the harder one pulled, the harder the other pulled. And with all their pulling, they were not getting any closer to their food.

Meanwhile, the knots got tighter and tighter.

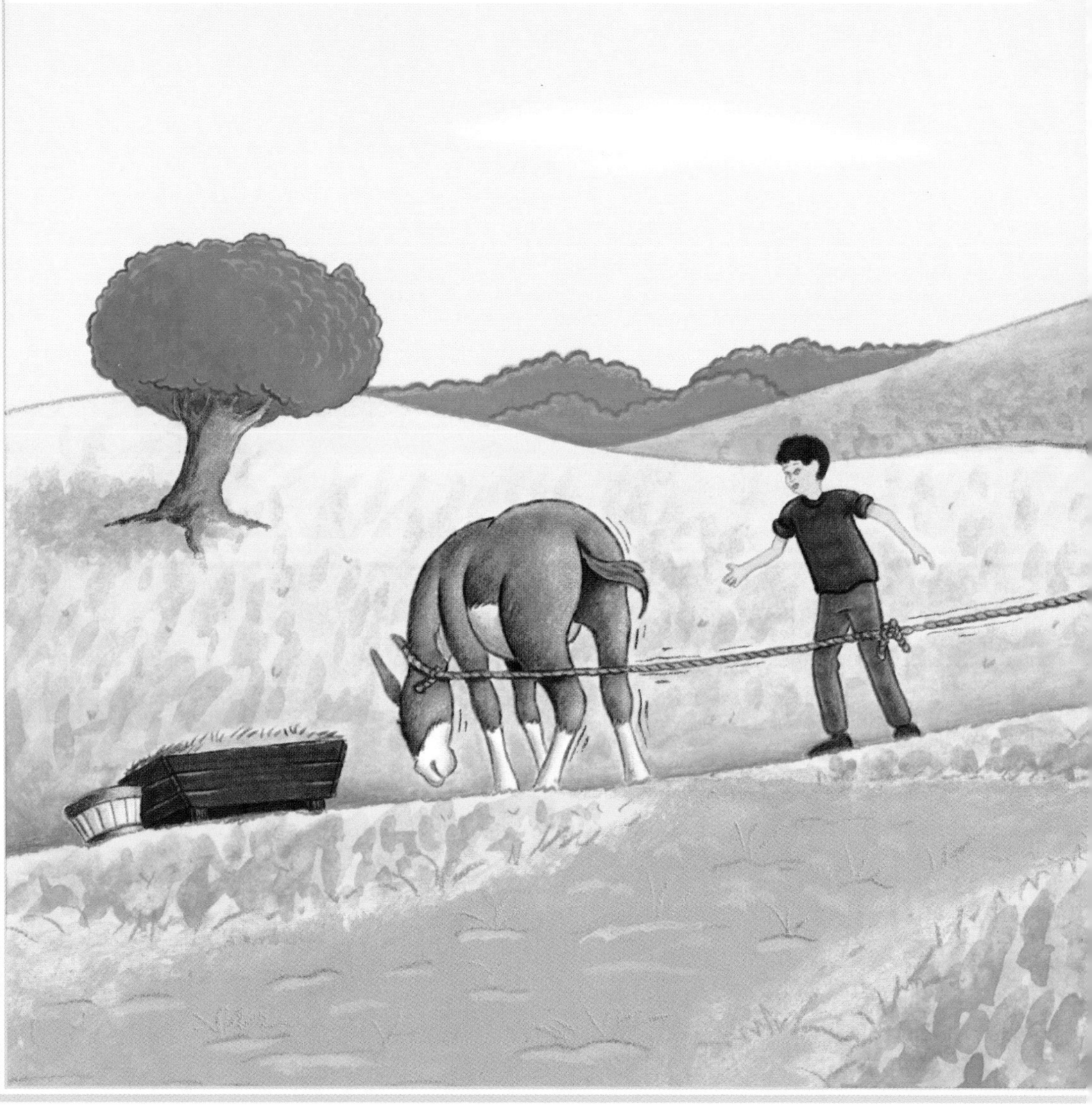

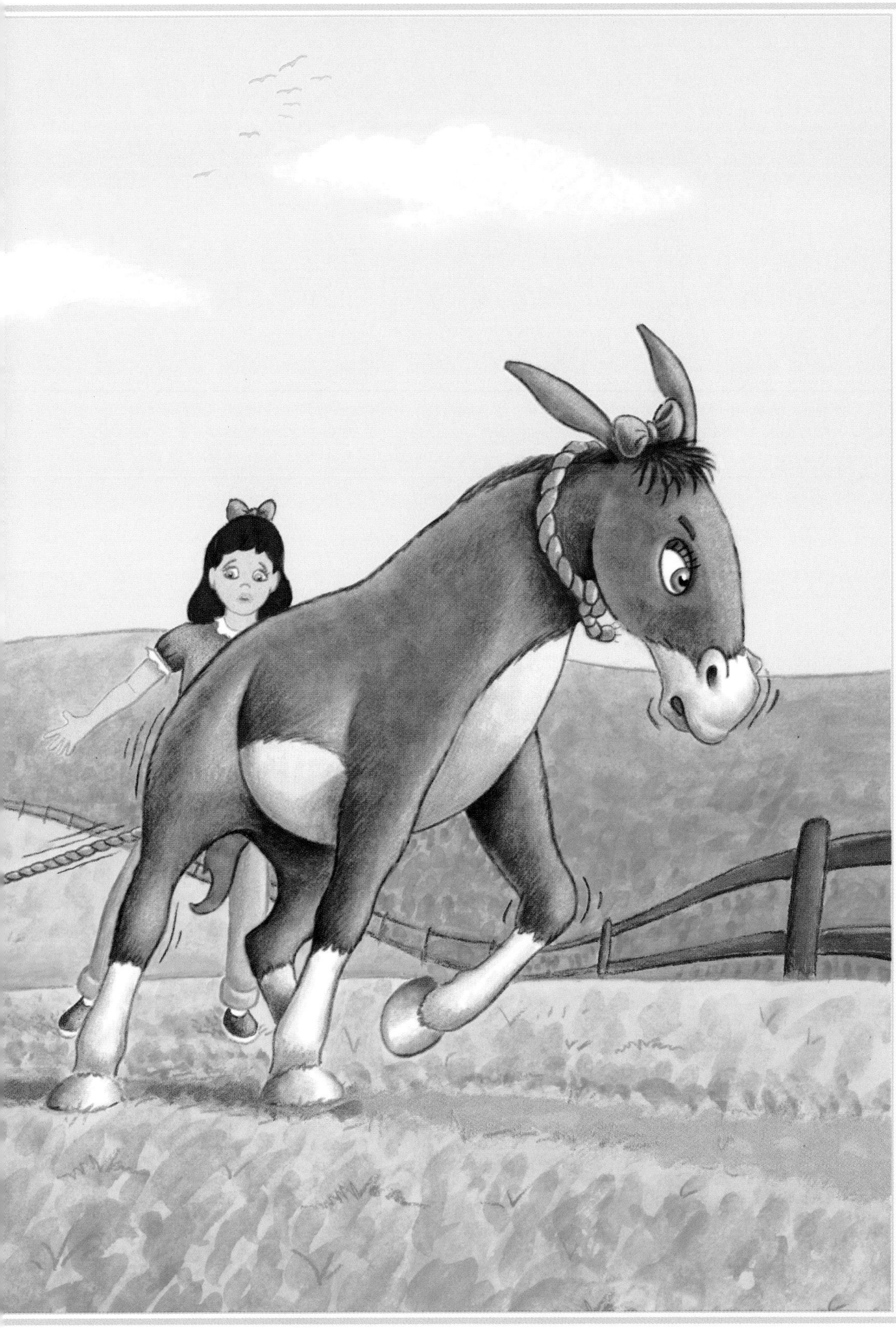

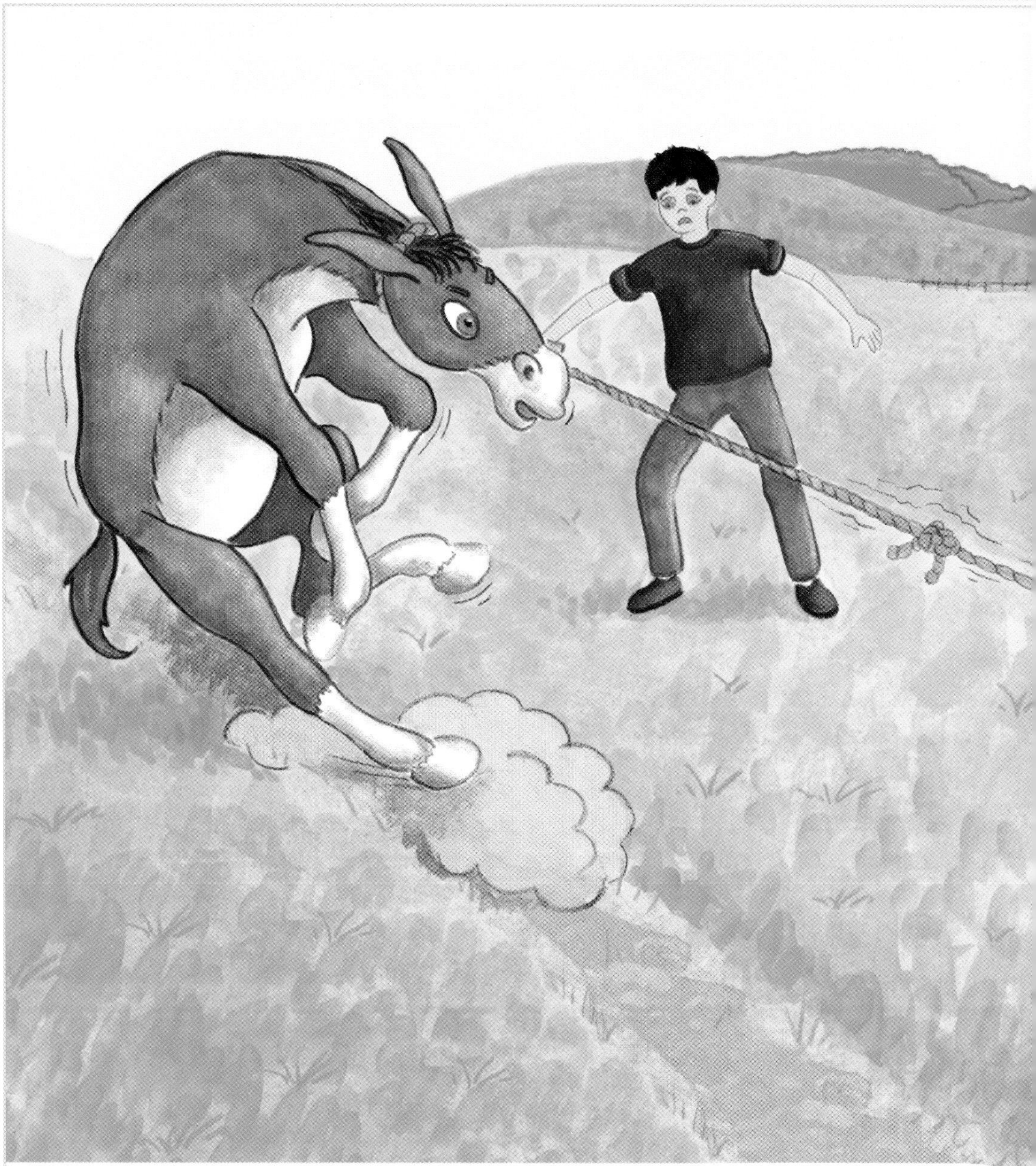

Thinking he was stronger, Bossy turned around backwards and began tugging. Not to be outdone, Stiffy did the same thing. They pulled...and pulled...and pulled! Still they were not getting any closer.

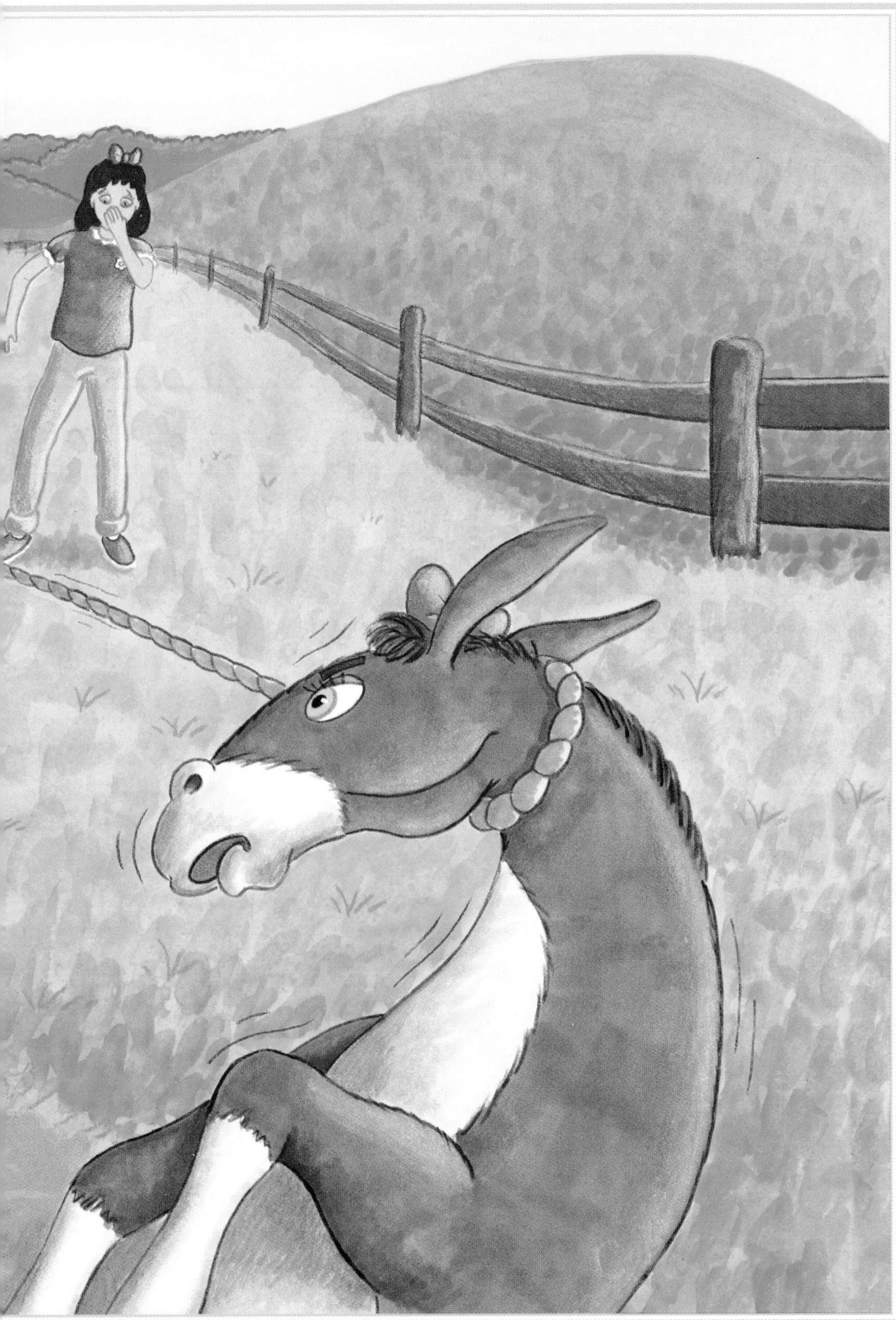

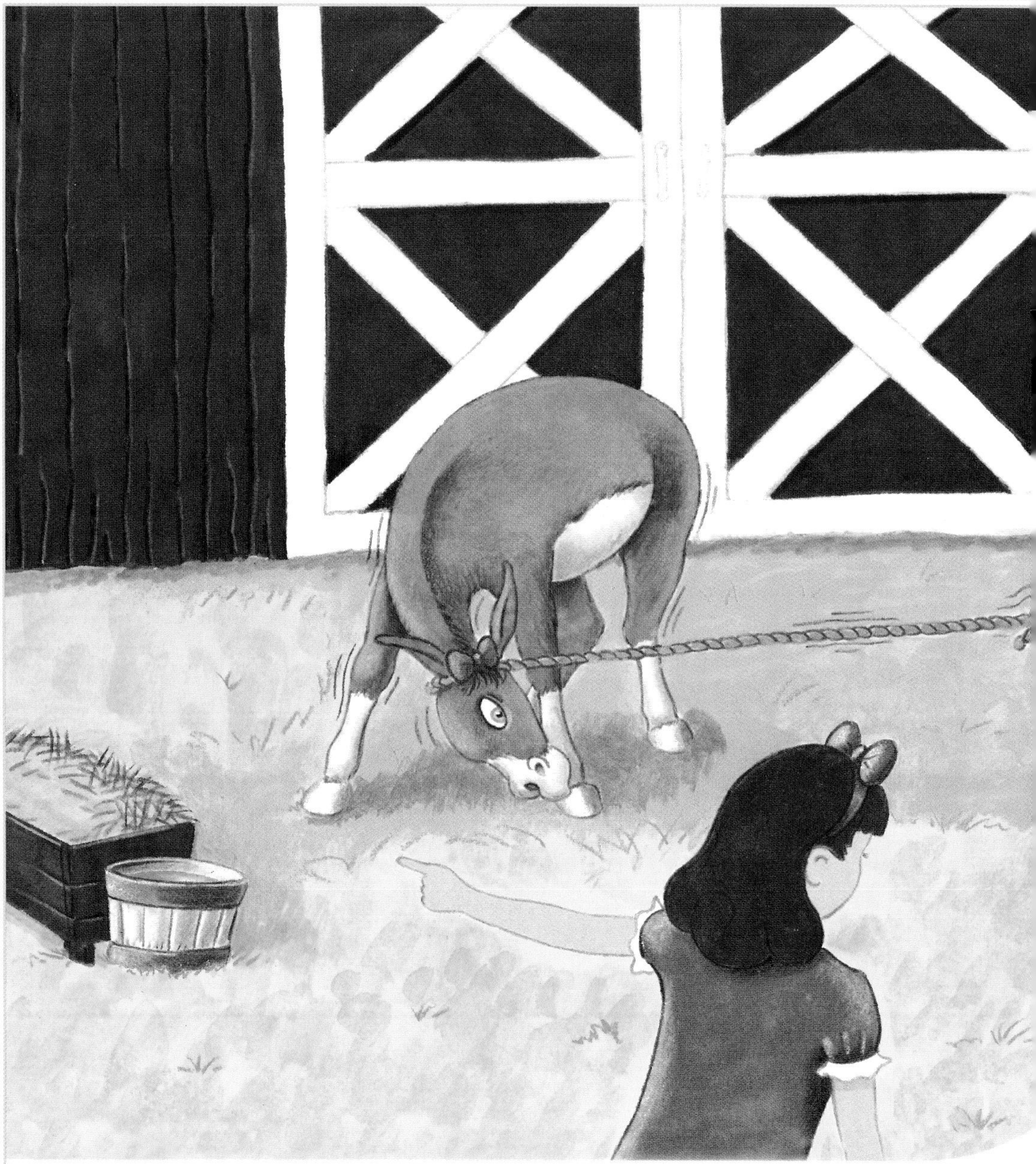

“Those knots are keeping them from eating!” shouted Benny.

“Why don’t you untie them?” Sally yelled back.

Benny tried, but the knots were much too tight.

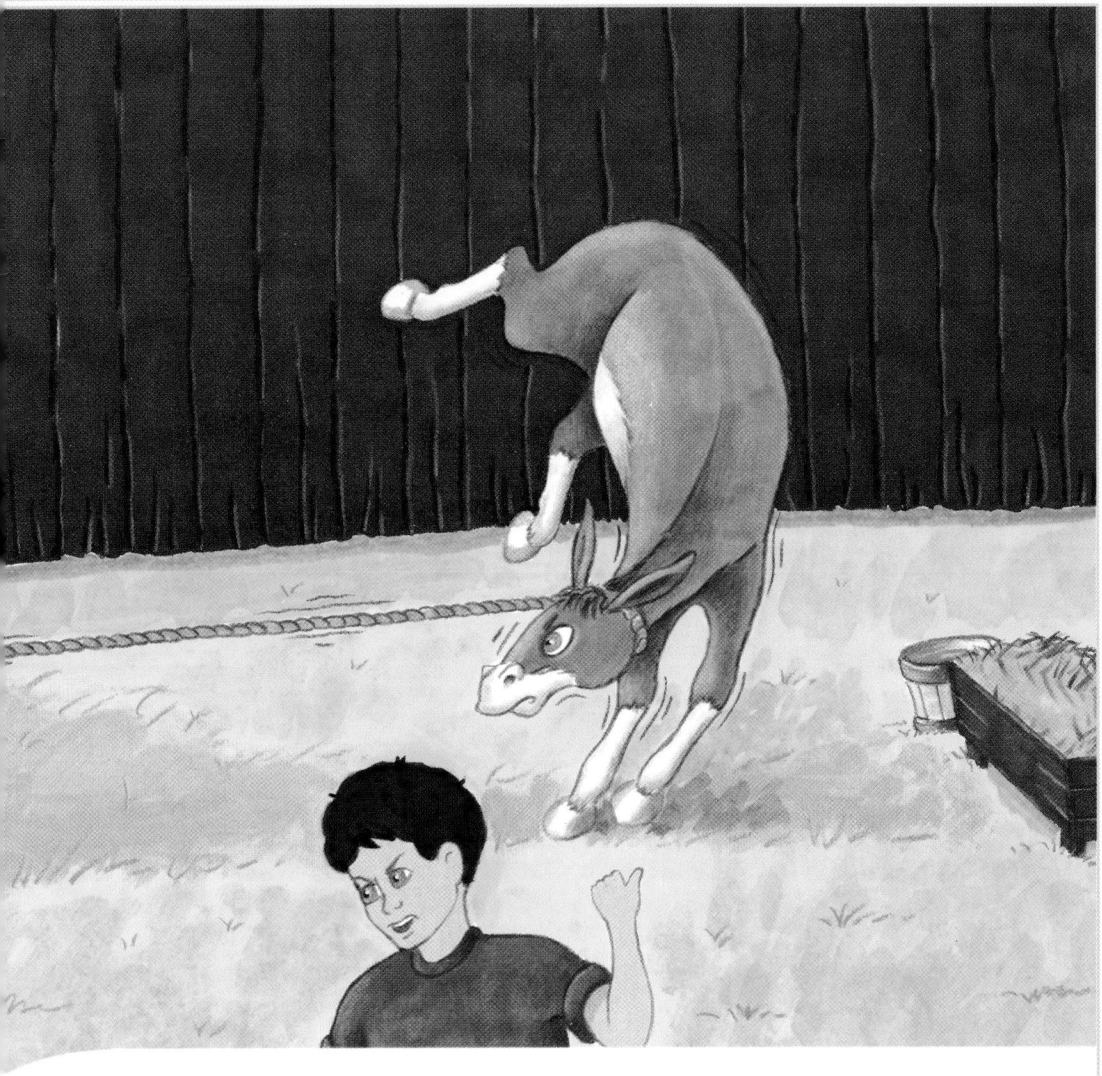

“Get Bossy to come to the middle so Stiffy can eat!” ordered Sally.

“No!” Benny argued. “Why should your mule eat first? You have Stiffy come to the middle so Bossy can eat first!”

Sally smiled and said, “Ladies first!”

“But my mule is older,” Benny snapped back. “The oldest should go first!”

Meanwhile, Bossy and Stiffy kept tugging.

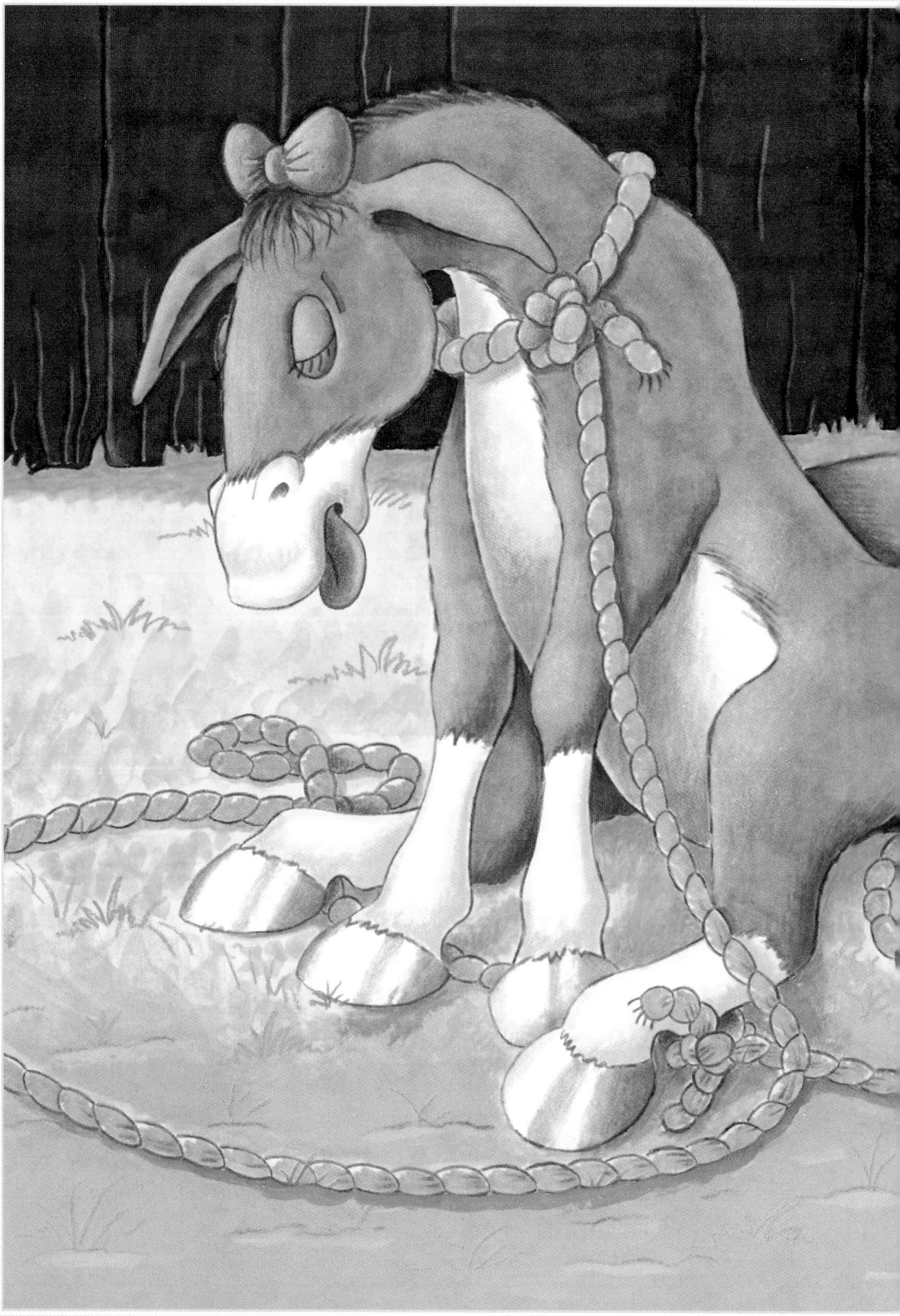

Bossy and Stiffy were now hot and tired... hungry and thirsty. They waddled back to the middle to rest.

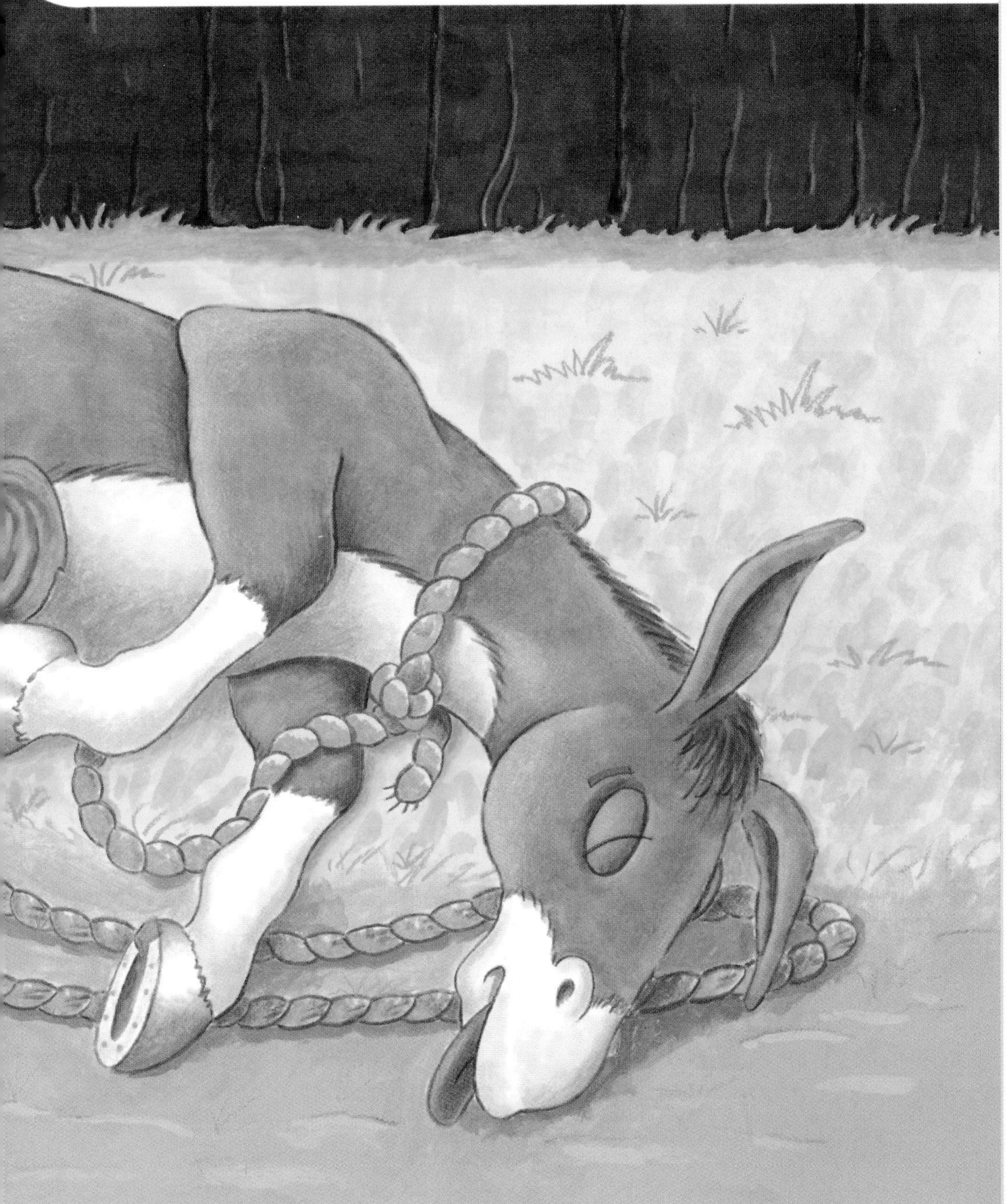

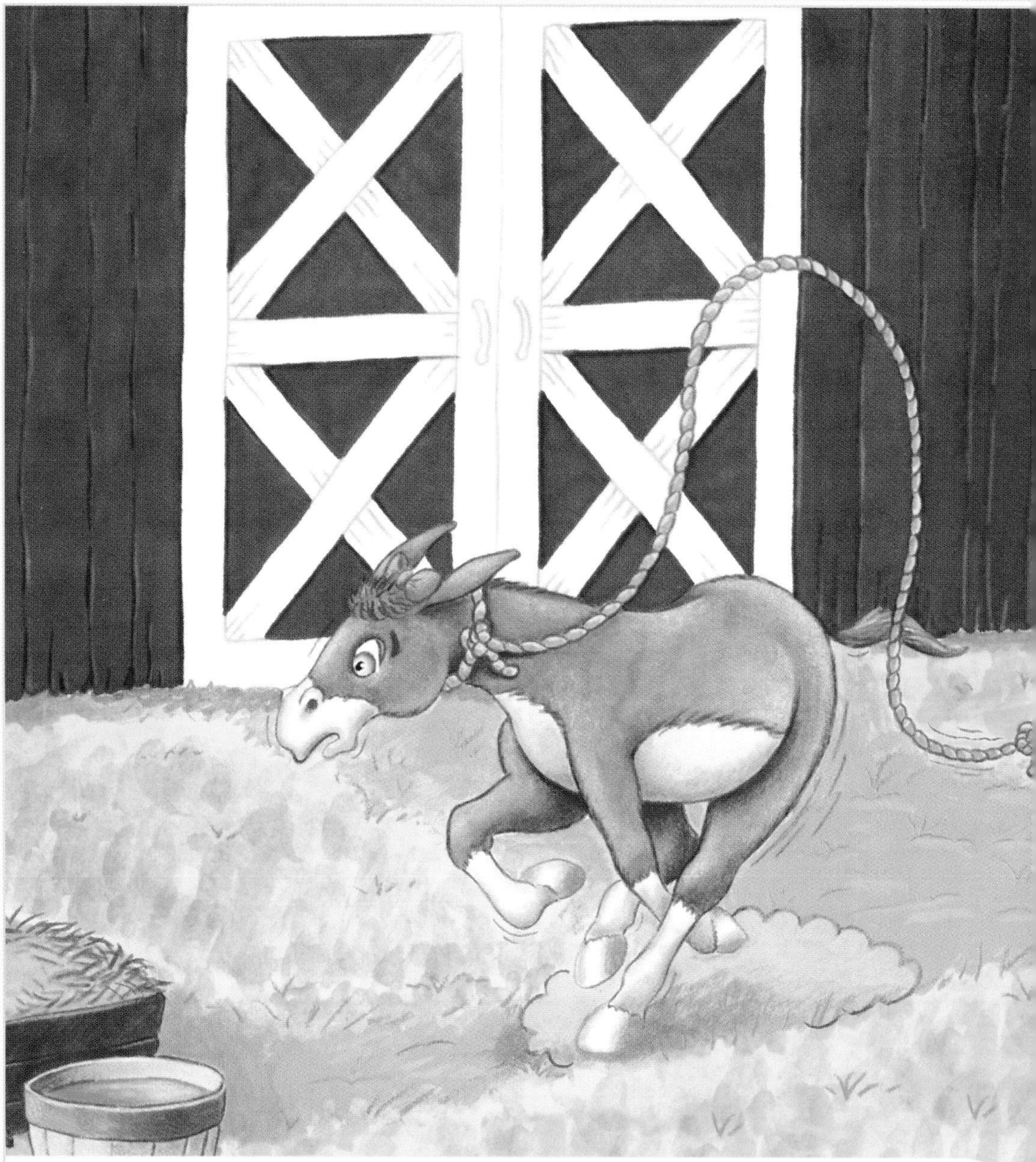

Bossy closed his eyes and let out a great big groan. "Ohhhh . . . !"

When Stiffy heard Bossy groaning, she got an idea. Quickly she jumped up and raced toward her food.

Bossy heard her jump. He was not about to let Stiffy eat her food first. In a flash he sprang to his feet and raced for his food.

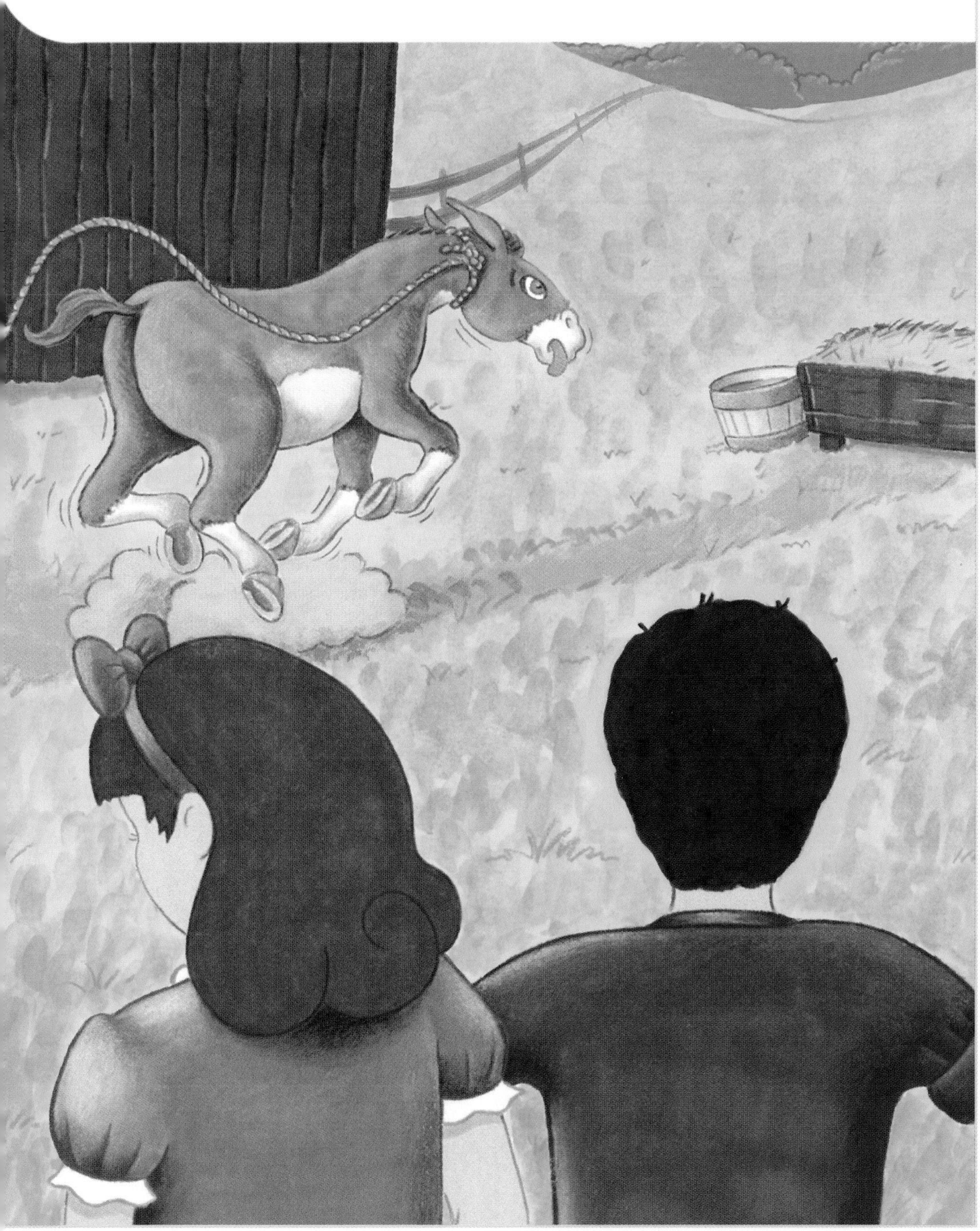

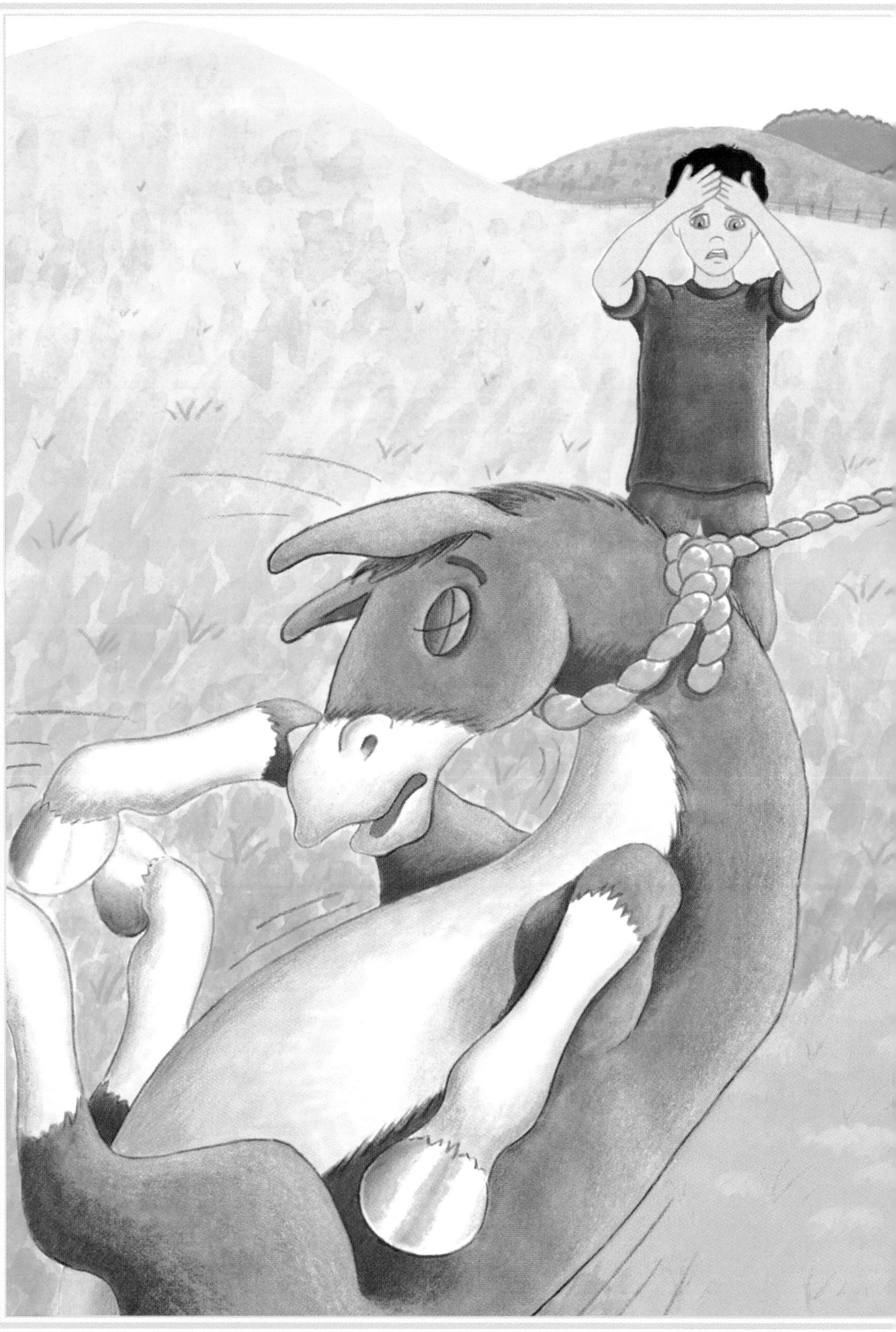

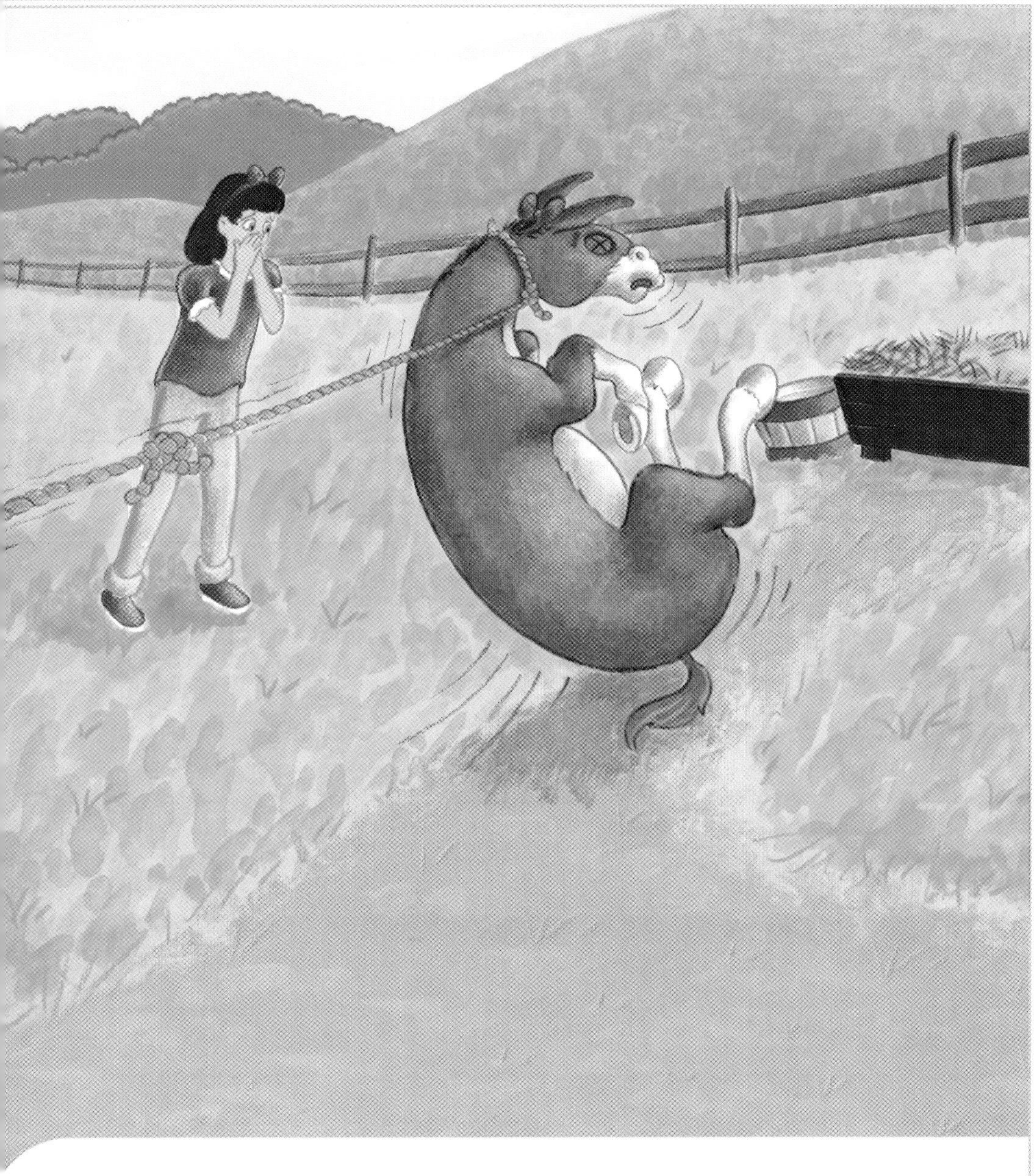

Bossy and Stiffy ran so fast that when they came to the end of the rope, they were yanked off their feet.

"Ouch!" shouted Benny as the mules hit the ground.

Sally gasped. "Are they alright?"

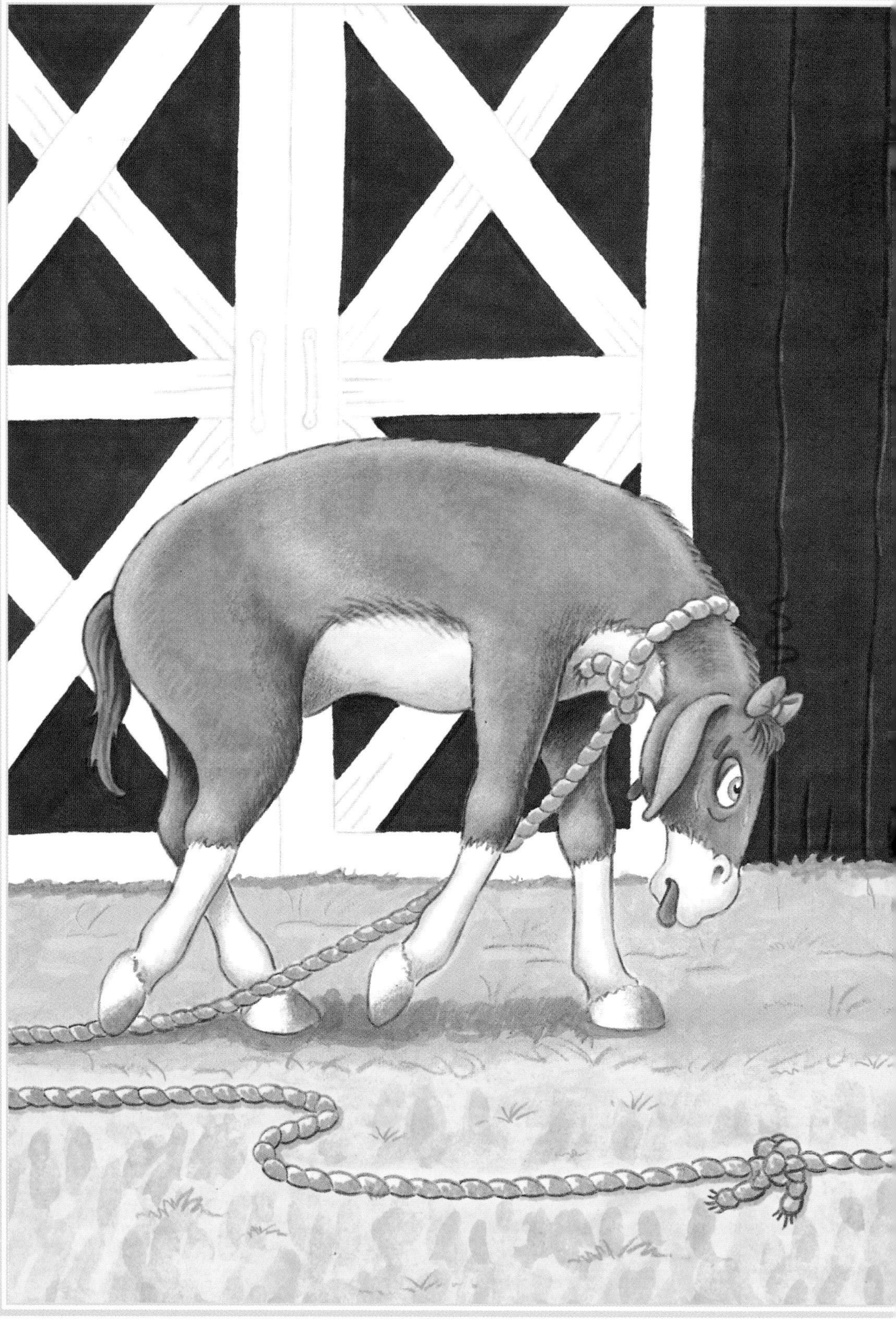

Bossy and Stiffy did not even utter a sound.

They slowly got up, shook their heads, and wobbled back to the middle.

They were now very hot and tired . . . and very hungry and thirsty. Nothing they did worked.

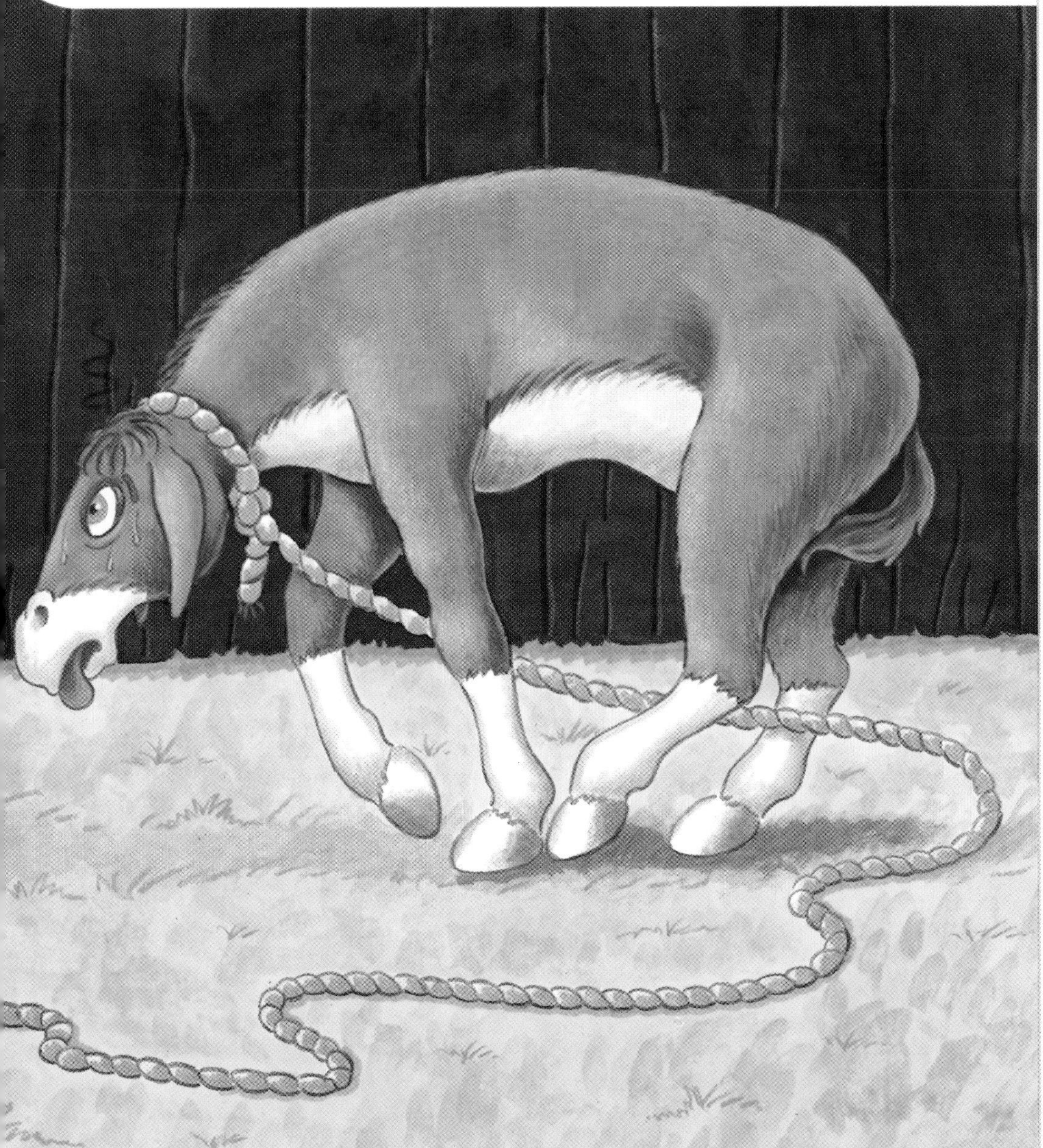

Benny headed for the barn. "I'm getting the cutters," he mumbled.

"Dad's not going to like it if you cut one of his ropes," warned Sally.

"We wouldn't have to if your stubborn mule would stay in the middle!" Benny argued.

"My mule?" asked Sally. "Why don't you have *your* stubborn mule stay in the middle?"

"If we can't agree," said Benny, "I'll just have to cut the rope."

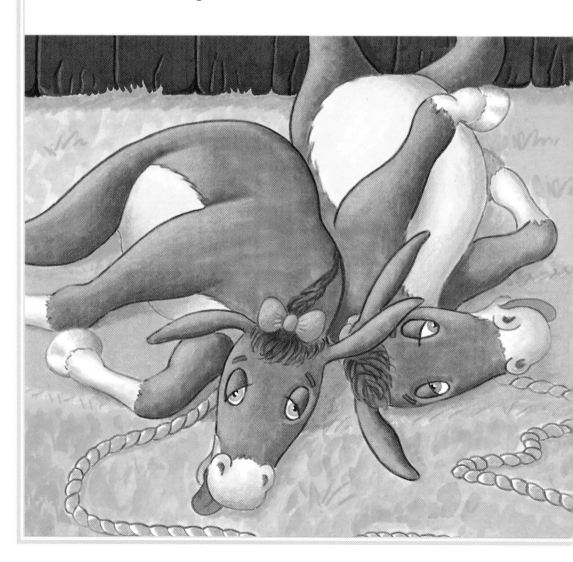

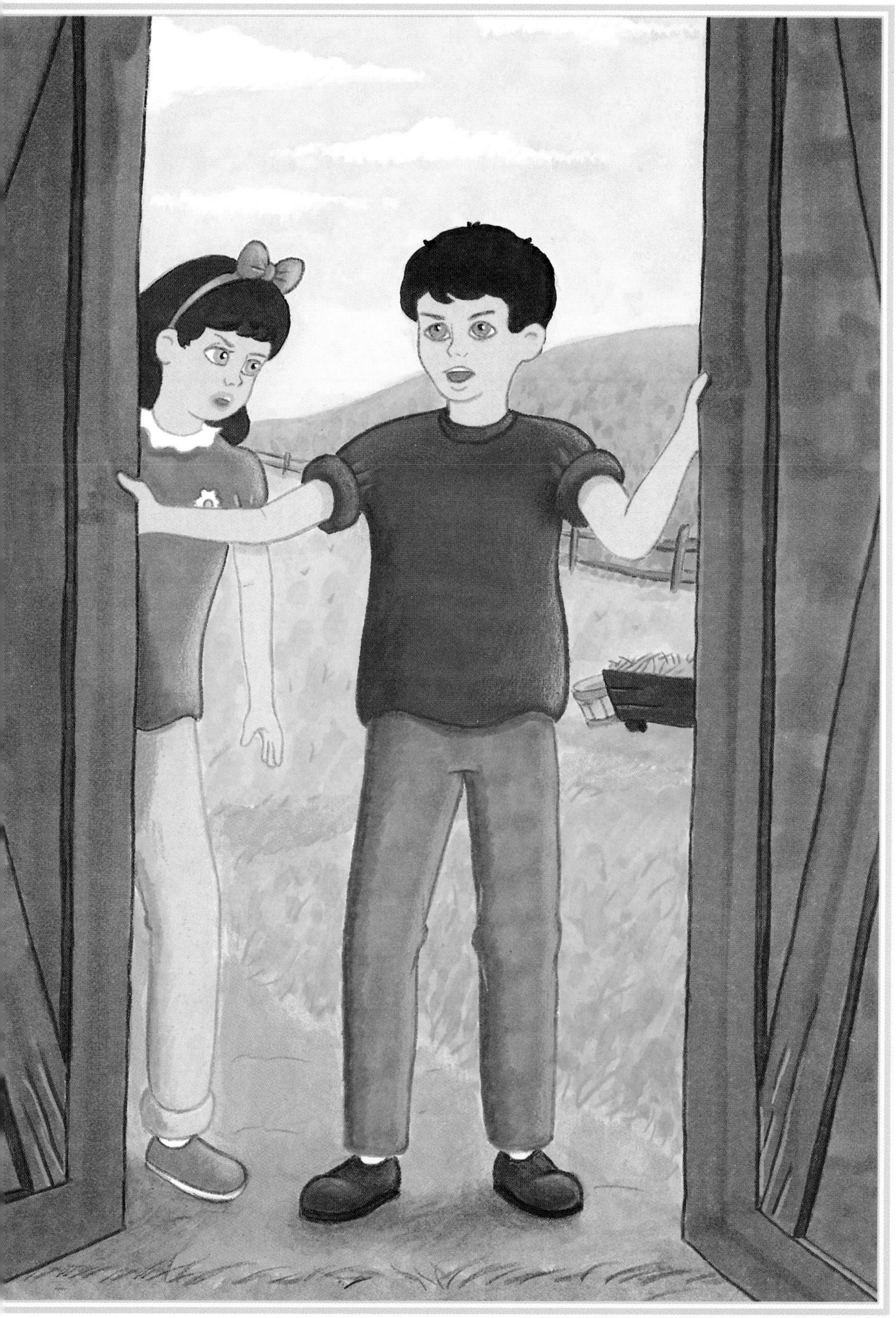

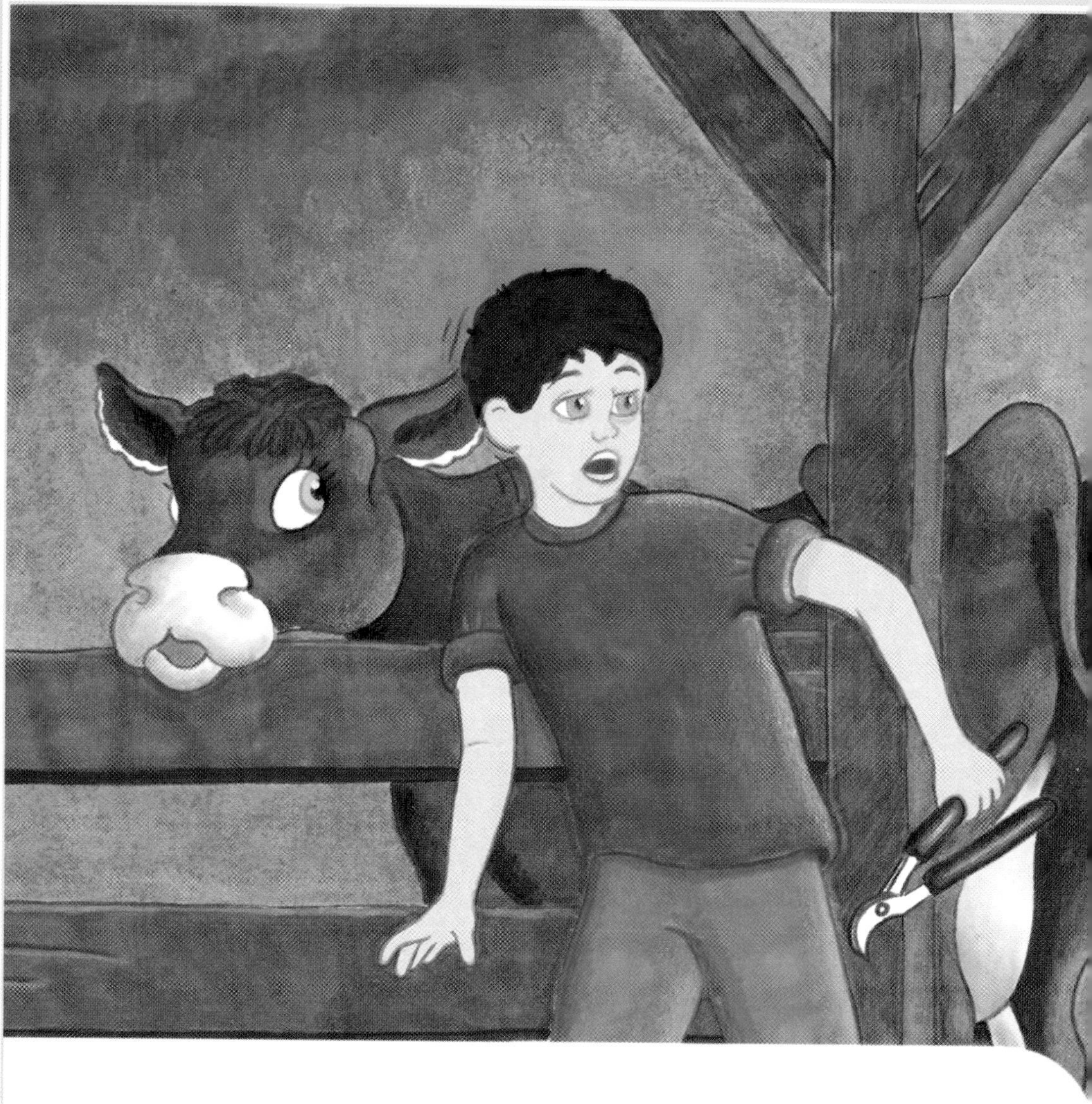

"You better not!" warned Sally. "That's a new rope."

"Well, I'm not going to let your mule eat first," said Benny. "That's just not fair!"

"And why should I let your mule eat first?" Sally argued. "That's not fair either!"

"Well then," snapped Benny, grabbing the cutters, "we'll just have to cut the—"

"Wait!" shouted Sally. "Look!"

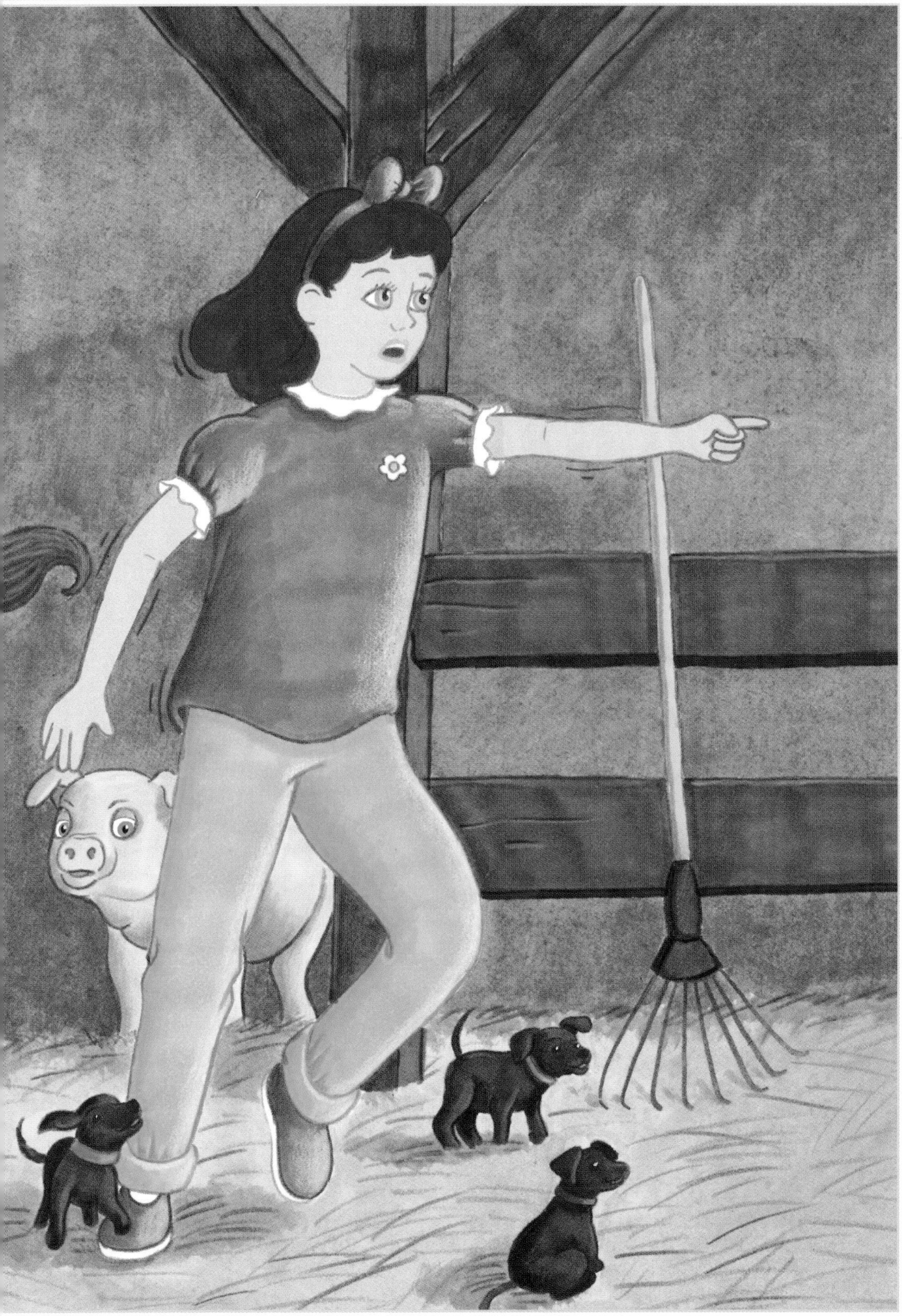

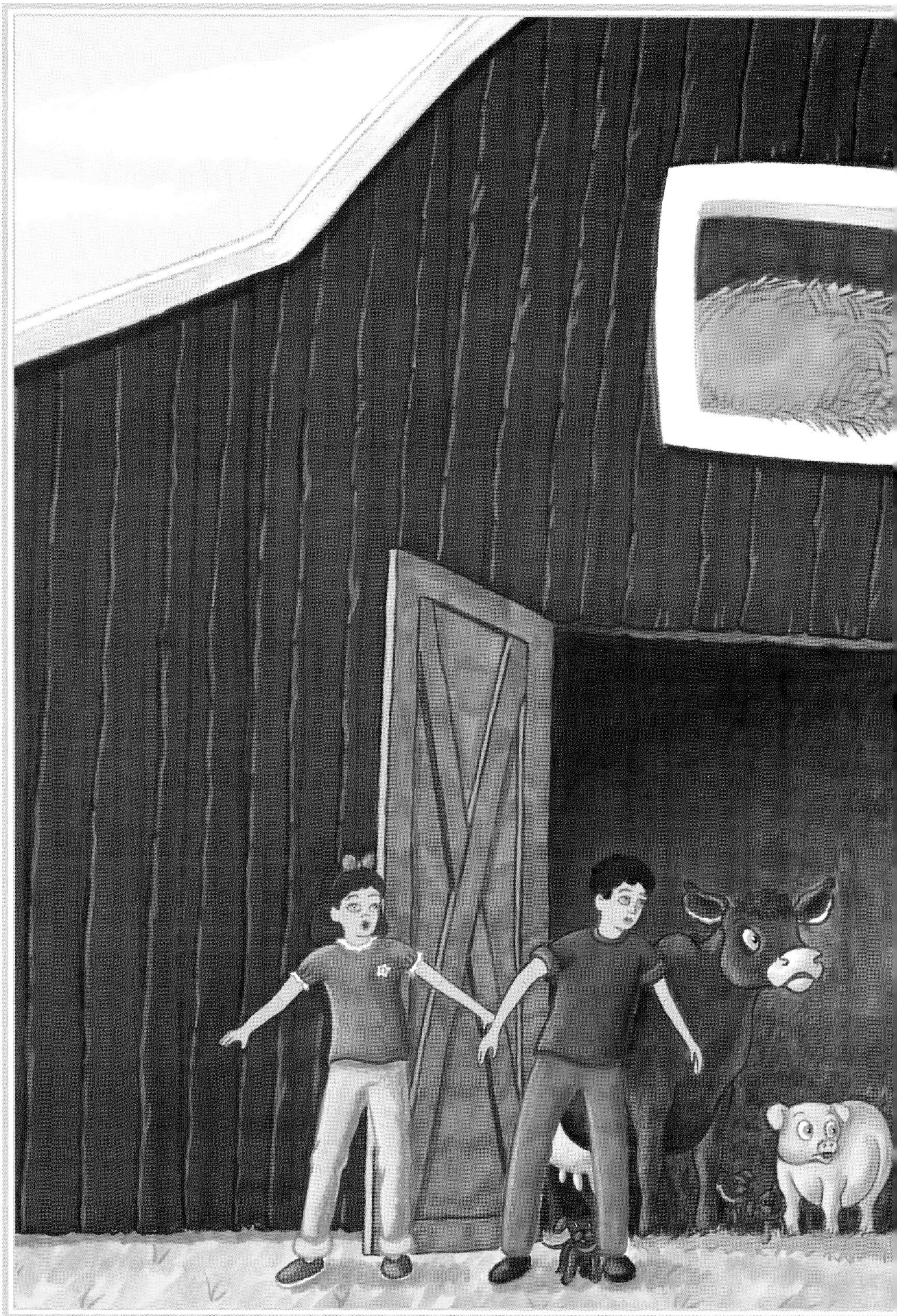

Sally and Benny ran toward the mules.

Bossy and Stiffy were still tied up in knots, but both mules were eating!

"How . . . how did they—?" muttered Benny.

"They're sharing!" Sally answered.

Bossy and Stiffy were happily bent over Stiffy's trough . . . gobbling up the hay.

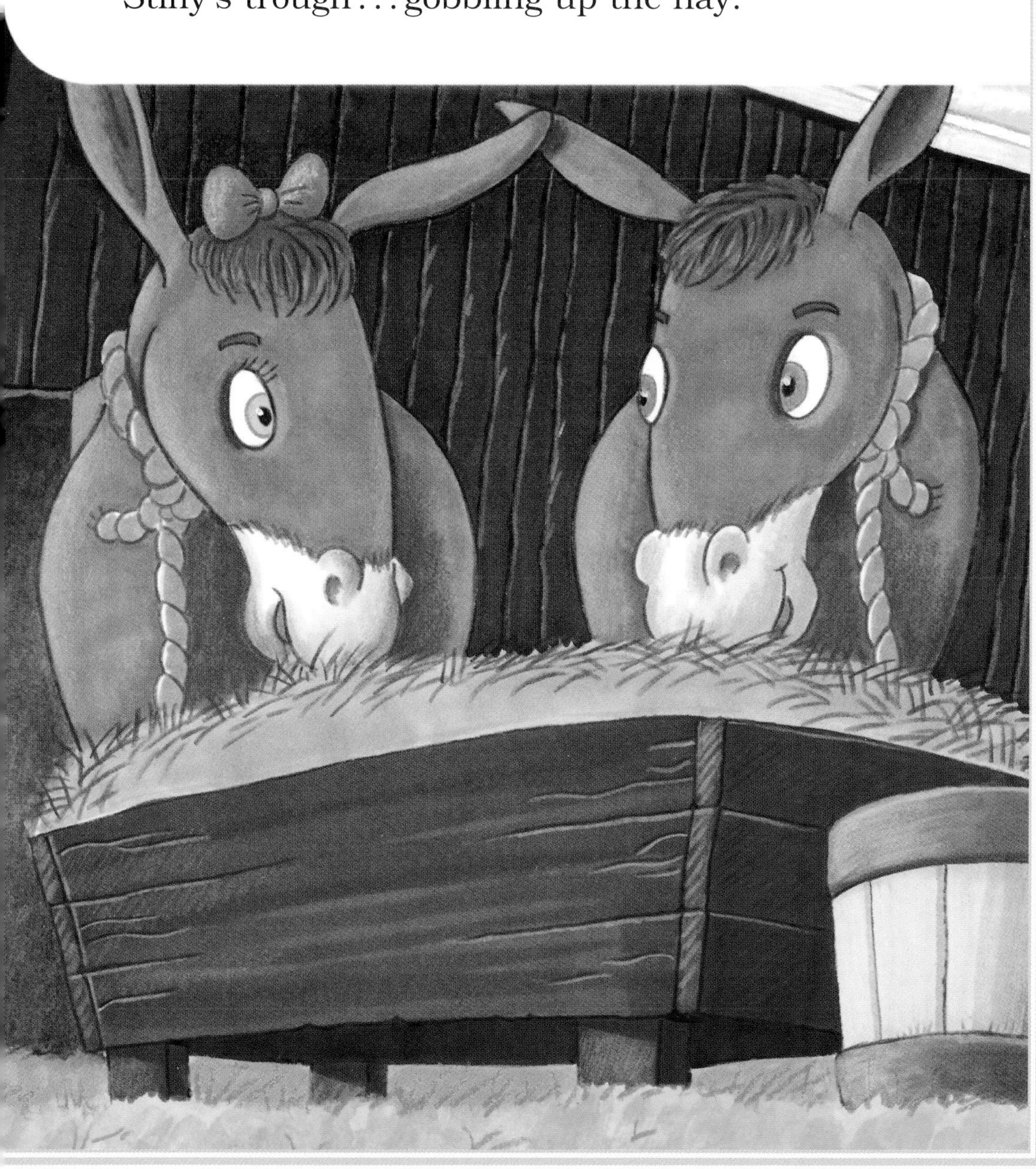

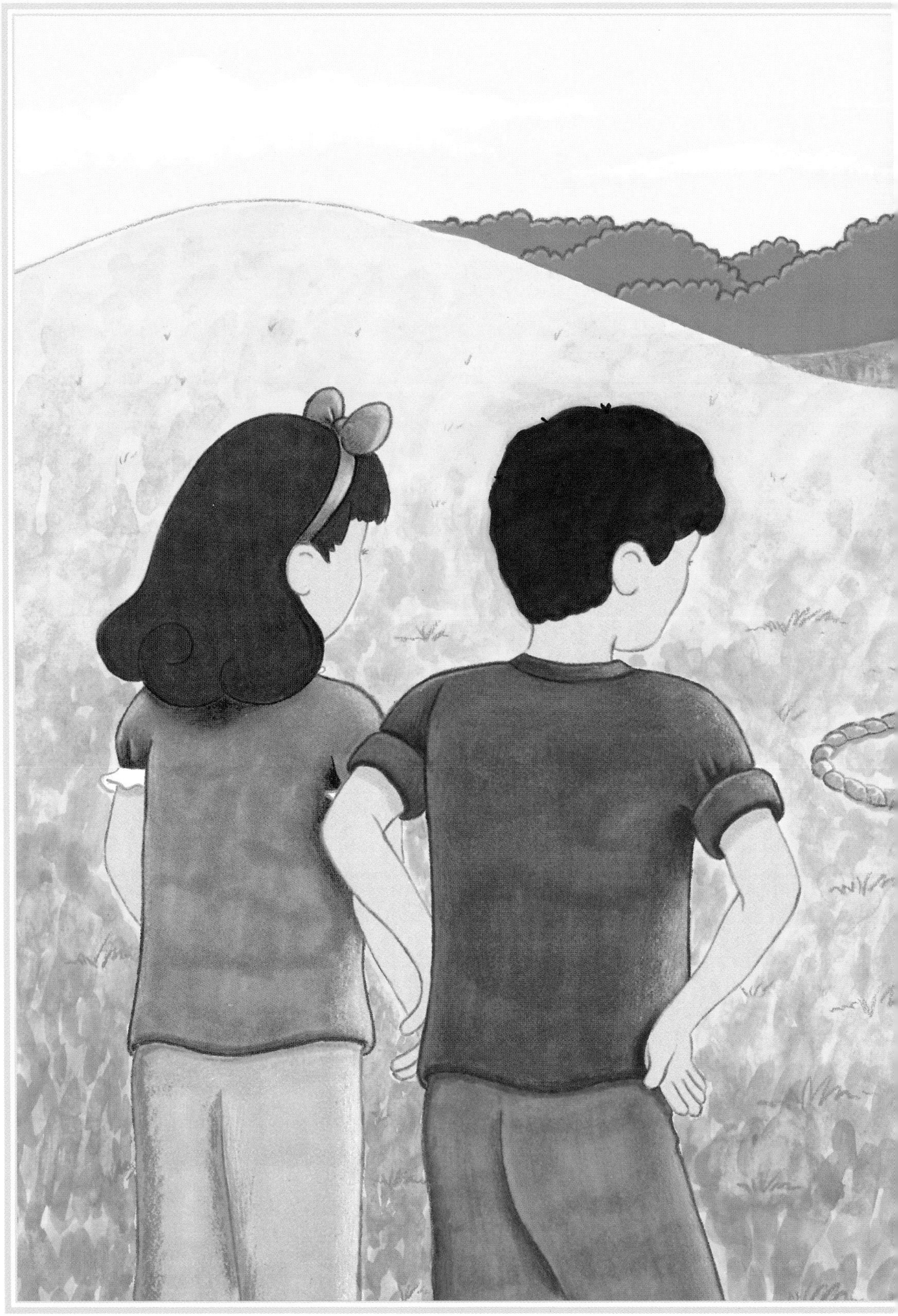

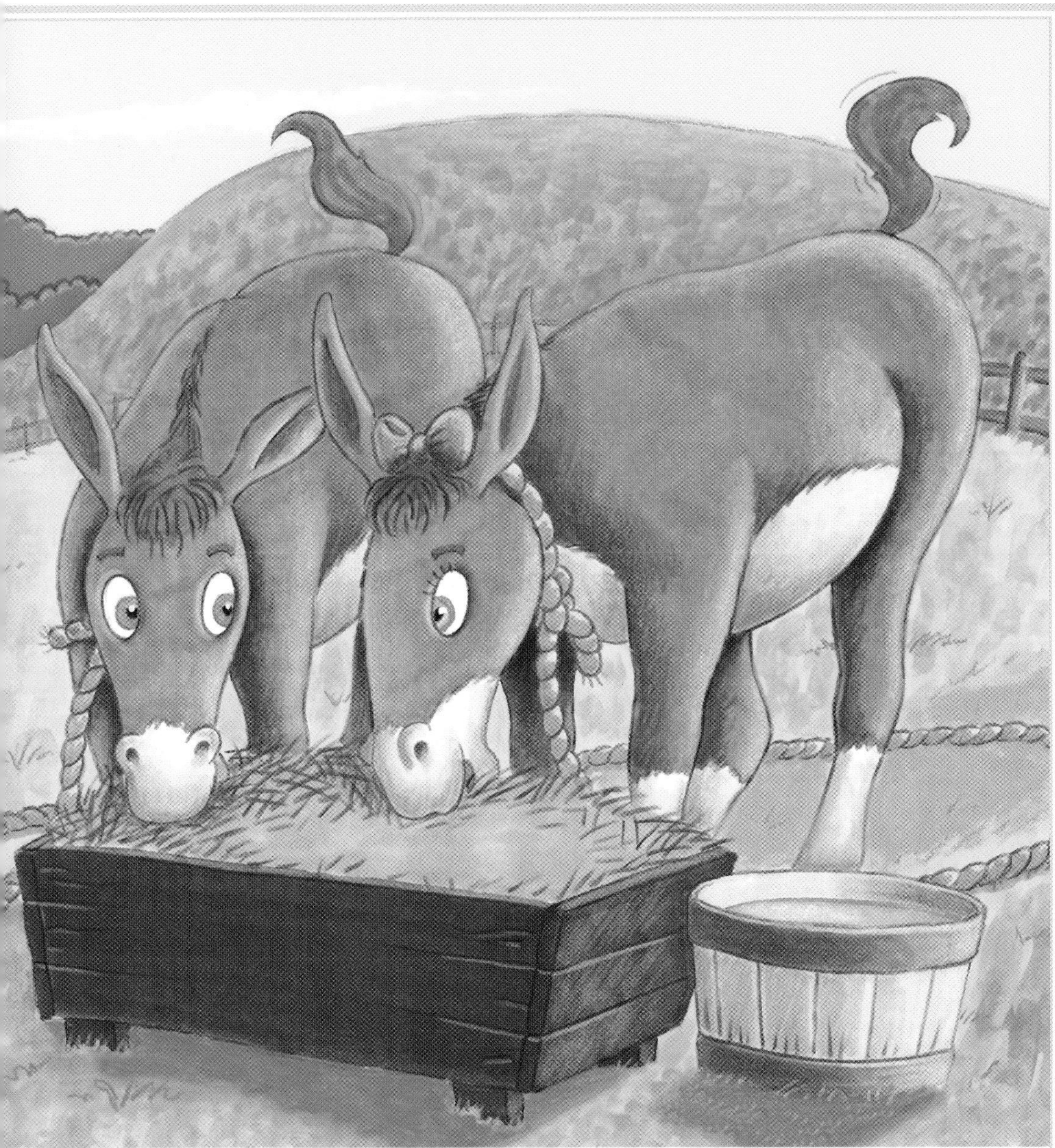

It did not take long before Stiffy's food was gone. Then the mules walked over to Bossy's pile of hay and began munching again.

"How simple!" said Benny, shaking his head. "They learned to share!"

"Why didn't we think of that?" asked Sally.

"Look at them," said Benny. "They look so happy."

"Of course they're happy," answered Dad from behind them.

"Dad! Mom!" Sally called. "Bossy and Stiffy are sharing!"

"That's the way it should be," said Mom.

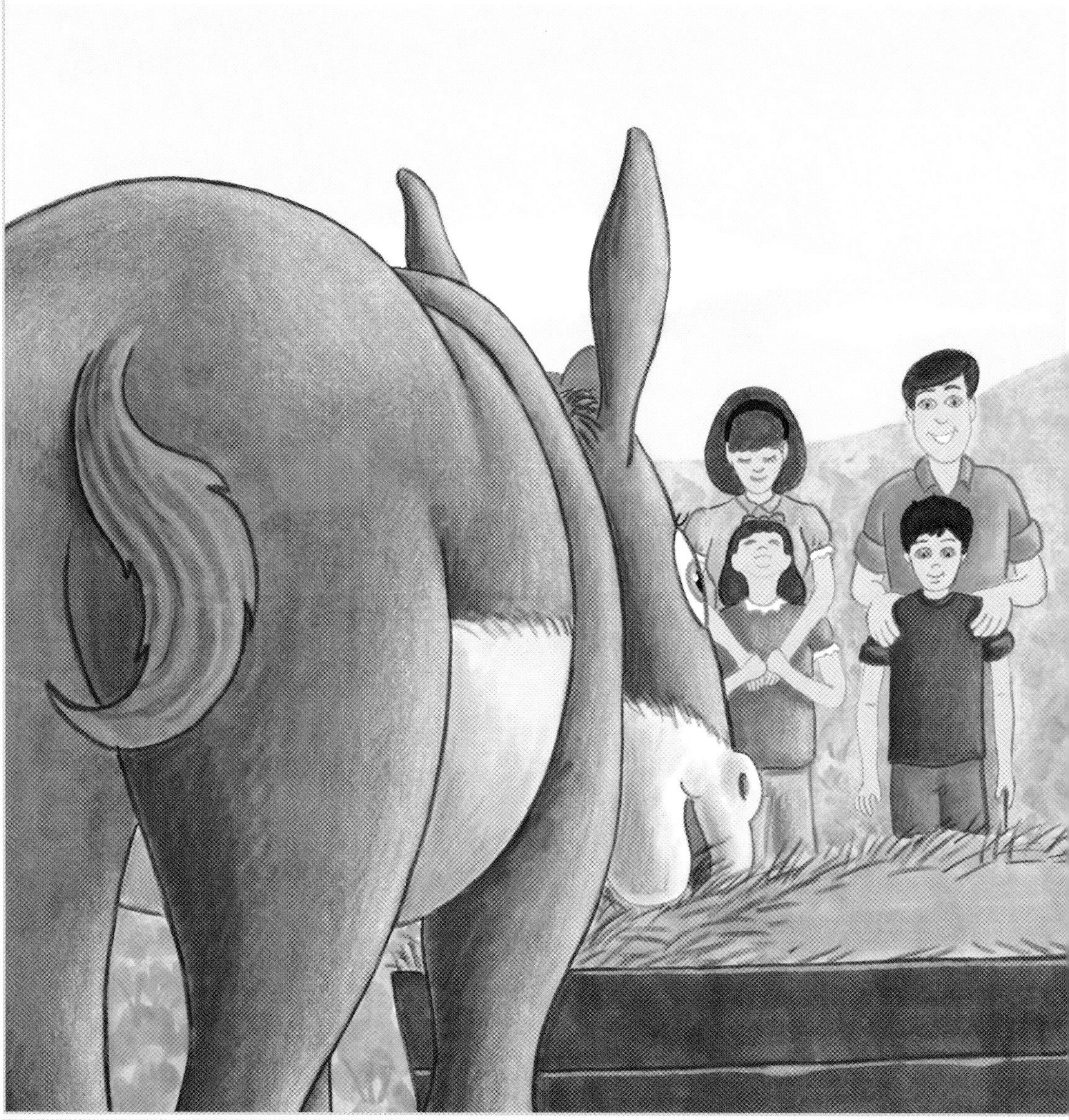

"They were tied up in knots," Benny explained, "and they couldn't eat or do anything."

"And they were so sad," added Sally, "until they decided to share—"

Sally paused as she remembered something Mom had said. "I guess it is true: Sharing does bring happiness!"

"It sure worked for them," said Benny.

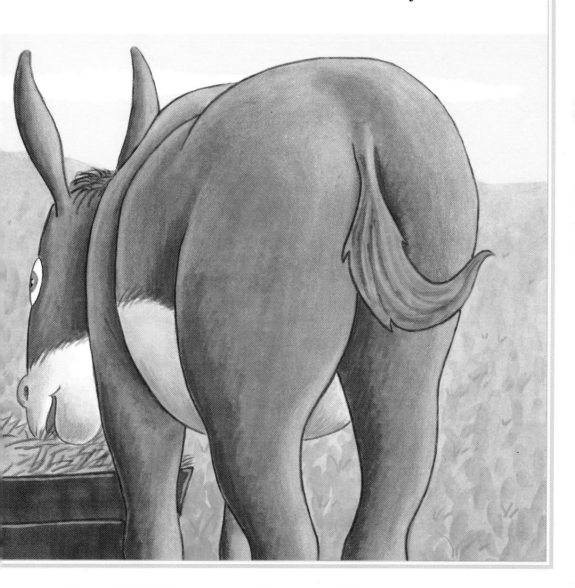

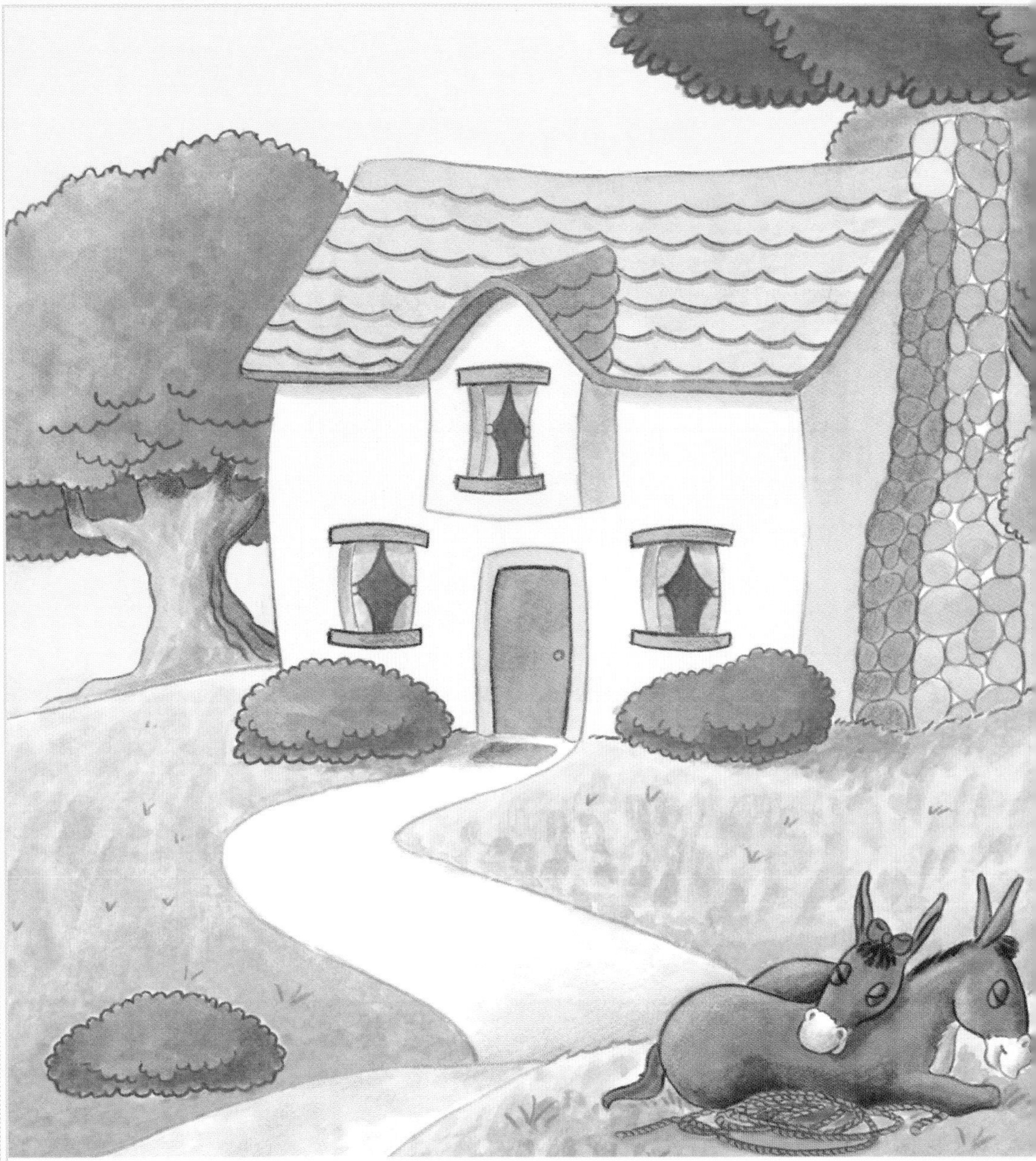

Dad untied the ropes, and Bossy and Stiffy laid down happily together and rested.

"Hooray!" shouted Benny and Sally as they shared a swing. "No more knots!"

And they were right.

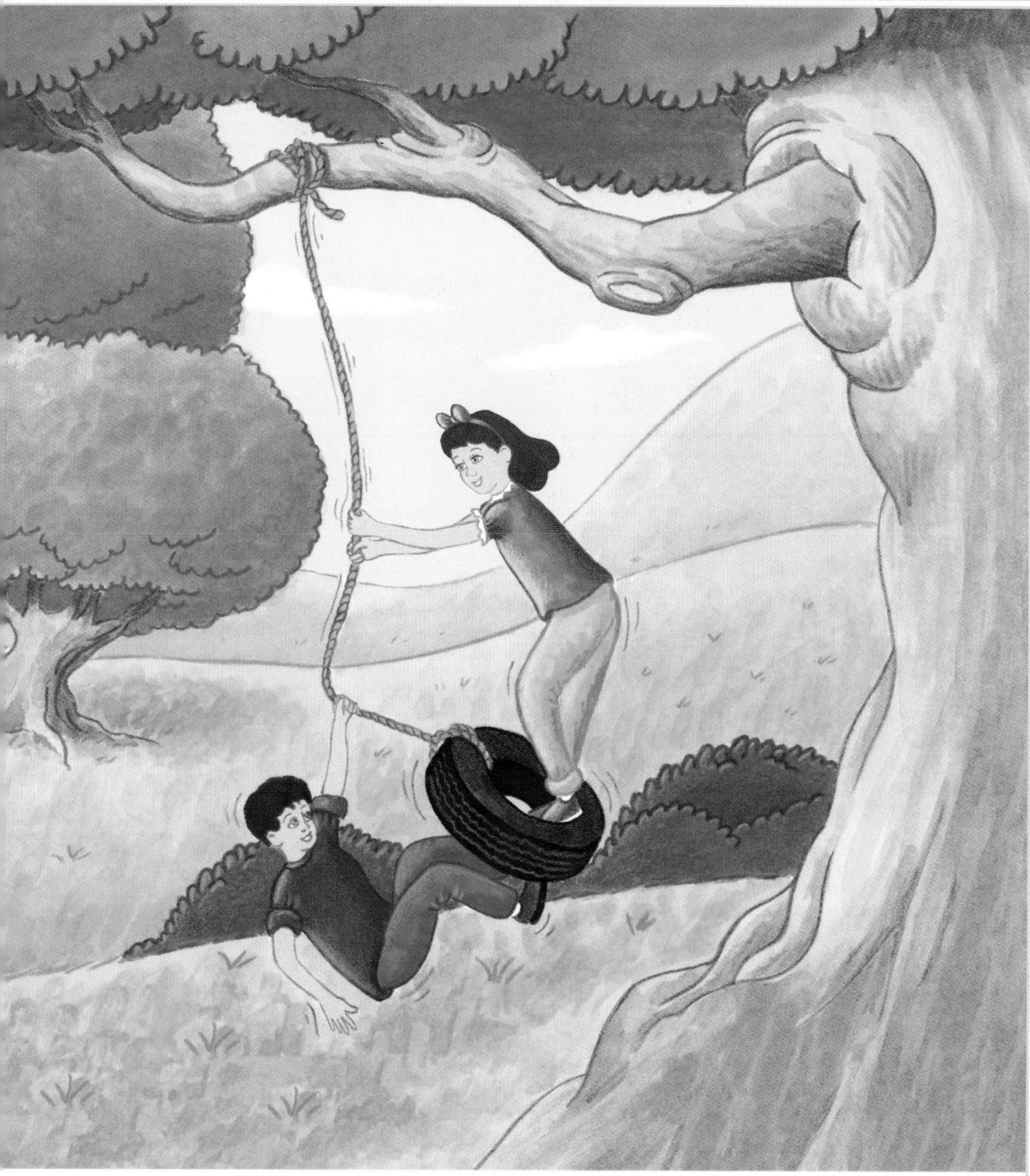

For though the lesson came from a couple of mules, Benny and Sally never forgot what they learned that day. Being selfish and stubborn makes you sad and gets you . . . *tied up in knots.*

But sharing brings happiness.